Praise for Elizabeth McCracken and
Here's Your Hat What's Your Hurry

"McCracken is as original a writer as they come."

—*The New Yorker*

"Strikes at the heart of the peculiarities and wonders of families and relationships. Elizabeth McCracken's stories are funny, tender, and disarming. They unfold beneath an aura of surreality, sporting oddball characters, surprising plots, weird but poignant logic, and uncommon sense . . . McCracken revels in the bizarre, but she's a true romantic, wonderfully attuned to the ordinary in the extraordinary and the miraculous in the everyday."

—*Booklist*

"The wonderful power of the human imagination emerges as a constant in this quirky, but accomplished, collection of tales. A power which transports its characters from the mundane to the heroic and symbolic."

—*The Times* (London)

"McCracken is a descendant of Anne Tyler, whose characters in the smallness of their lives project large themes."

—*Austin American-Statesman*

"Wonderful . . . All the stories in this offbeat collection live up to the promise of their titles . . . Although McCracken has filled her stories with a cast of oddballs, she has created such compelling lives for them that she moves beyond our curiosity to gain our sympathy."

—*Library Journal*

"McCracken is not merely a born raconteur; she is also an assured stylist and an astute student of human nature . . . a wise and compassionate reader of the human heart."

—*Publishers Weekly*

Here's Your Hat What's Your Hurry

STORIES BY

ELIZABETH McCRACKEN

AVON BOOKS NEW YORK

Some of the stories in this work were originally published in *Epoch, Ex Libris, The Michigan Quarterly Review*, and *Story*.

AVON BOOKS, INC.
1350 Avenue of the Americas
New York, New York 10019

Front cover illustration by Sean Beavers
Inside back cover author photo by Sam McCracken
Published by arrangement with Random House, Inc.
Visit our website at **http://www.AvonBooks.com**
Library of Congress Catalog Card Number: 92-56833
ISBN: 0-380-73079-0

First Avon Books Trade Printing: October 1997

Printed in the U.S.A.

OPM 10 9 8 7 6 5 4 3 2

For Ruth Jacobson,
who is my grandmother,
among many other things.

CONTENTS

Here's Your Hat What's Your Hurry

IT'S BAD LUCK TO DIE

MAYBE YOU WONDER HOW a Jewish girl from Des Moines got Jesus Christ tattooed on her three times: ascending on one thigh, crucified on the other, and conducting a miniature apocalypse beneath the right shoulder. It wasn't religion that put them there; it was Tiny, my husband. I have a Buddha round back, too. He was going to give me Moses parting the Red Sea, but I was running out of space. Besides, I told him, I was beginning to feel like a Great Figures in Religion comic book.

He got dreamy-eyed when he heard that. "Brigham Young," he said. "And some wives."

I told him: "Tiny, I've got no room for a polygamist."

Tiny himself had been married three times before he met me, one wife right after the other. I only had him, the one, and he's been dead six months now.

I met Tiny the summer I graduated high school, 1965, when I was eighteen and he was forty-nine. My cousin Babs, who was a little wild, had a crazy boyfriend (the whole family was worried about it) and he and some of his buddies dared her to get tattooed. She called me up and told me she needed me there and that I was not to judge, squawk, or faint at the sight of blood. She knew none of that was my style, anyhow.

We drove to Tiny's shop over on East 14th because that's where Steve, the crazy boy, had got the panther that had a toehold on his shoulder. The shop was clean and smelled of antiseptic; Babs and I were disappointed. Sheets of heavy paper in black dime-store frames hung on the walls—flash sheets—arranged by theme: one had Mickey Mouse and Woody Woodpecker; another, a nurse in a Red Cross cap and a geisha offering a drink on a tray. A big flash by the door had more ambitious designs: King Kong and Cleopatra on the opposite sides of one page, looking absentmindedly into each other's eyes.

Tiny was set up on a stool in back, smoking a cigarette, an itty-bit of a man next to a Japanese screen. He was wearing a blue dress shirt with the cuffs turned back, and his hands and arms were covered with blue-black lines: stars across the knuckles, snakes winding up under the sleeves. The wide flowered tie that spread out over his chest and stomach might've been right on a big man, but on Tiny it looked like an out-of-control garden. His pants were white and wrinkled, and there was a bit of blue ink at the knee; a suit jacket, just as wrinkled, hung on the coat rack in back.

He eyed our group, scowled at Steve and his two friends, and solemnly winked at me and Babs.

"So," he said. "Who's the one?"

"Me," Babs said, trying to sound tough. She told him what she wanted: a little red-and-black bow on her tush. He asked her if she were old enough; she got out her wallet and showed him her driver's license.

Steve and his friends were buzzing around the shop, looking at the flash and tapping the ones they really liked.

"Keep your hands off the designs, boys," said Tiny. "I can't tattoo a fingerprint." He turned to Babs. "Okay. Come back of the screen." There was something a little southern in his voice, but I couldn't pick out what it was. He jumped off the stool, and I saw that he was about a full foot shorter than me. I'm six feet tall, have been since eighth grade. I looked right down on top of his slick black hair.

We all started to follow him. Tiny looked at us and shook his head.

"You boys have to stay out here."

"I'm her boyfriend," said Steve. "I've seen it before, and I'm paying."

"If you've seen it before, you'll see it again, so you don't need to now. Not in my shop, anyhow. You—" he pointed at me "—come around to testify I'm a gentleman."

He beckoned us back of the screen to a padded table, the kind you see in doctors' offices, only much lower. Tiny turned around politely while Babs lowered her blue jeans and clambered up. He spun back, frowned, pulled down just the top of her yellow flowered underwear like he was taking fat off a chicken, and tapped her. "Right here's where you want it?"

"That's fine."

"Honey, is it fine, or is it what you want?"

Babs twisted to look, careful not to catch his eye. "That's what I want."

He squirted her with antiseptic, got a razor and shaved the area good. I sat on a folding chair across from them.

Tiny loosened his tie, slipped it off, and hung it, still knotted, on a peg on the wall. "Hey Stretch," he said, looking at me. "What's your name?"

"Lois."

"Lois. Like Louise?" He rolled his shirtsleeves up further. Babs was holding on to the table like a drowning sailor, and Tiny hadn't even got the needle out yet.

"Lois," I answered, and fast, because I had to talk to him over Babs's hindquarters and that made me a little self-conscious, "after my Uncle Louis. I was going to be named Natalie, after my Uncle Nathan, but then Louis died and Mom liked him better anyhow."

"My name is Tiny. No story there but the obvious." He picked up an electric needle from a workbench and hunted for the right pot of color.

"I'm Babs," said Babs, reaching around for a handshake. Tiny was looking elsewhere, and he dipped the needle in some black ink and flipped it on. "For Barbara?" he asked, setting into her skin.

"A-a-a-a-bigail. Ouch." She gripped the table.

"Honey," said Tiny, "this doesn't hurt. I got you where you're good and fleshy. Might sting a little, but it doesn't hurt."

"Okay," said Babs, and she sounded almost convinced.

"For Abraham," I said suddenly. "Abigail after Abraham."

"Pretty girls named after men," said Tiny, taking a cloth and wiping some ink off of Babs so he could see what he was doing. "Thought that only happened in the South."

Looking back, it seems like he took an hour working on Babs, but now I know it couldn't have been more than ten minutes. He looked up at me from time to time, smiling or winking. I thought that he was just one of those flirty types, one of those bold little guys, and that if he had been looking at Babs in the face instead of where he was looking at her, he would've flirted with her the same. Years later he told me that he was bowled over by all those square inches of skin, how I was so big and still not fat. "I fell for you right away," he said.

Up until then, I'd always thought it was only sensible to fall in love with tall men so that I wouldn't look like so much of a giantess. That way we could dance in public, in scale, no circus act. It didn't matter, though: I never had a date all through high school, couldn't dance a step. I spent my time in movie houses, because most movie stars looked pretty tall, even if it was only a trick of the camera, a crate under their feet in love scenes.

Tiny, no doubt, no tricks about it, was short, but he charmed me from the start. His charm was as quick and easy as his needle, and he could turn it on and off the same way. On the Tuesday afternoons I visited him before we got married, I saw all types jangle the bell on the front door as they pushed it open: big men, skinny kids, nervous couples gambling on love forever. Most of them asked the same thing: "Does it hurt?" To people who rubbed him wrong, he'd say, "If you're worried about it, I guess you don't really want one"; to those he liked, chiefly the women, he'd drawl, "I could make you smile while I do it." He could, too; he could tell your background by the feel of your skin, and would talk about ridiculous things—baseball scores, recipes for homemade beer, the sorry state of music—anything but the business at hand.

He could even charm my mother, who, on meeting Tiny, this little man only two years younger than her, was grieved to discover she liked him.

When he was finished with Babs, he put on a bandage and handed her a little white card that said *How To Take Care Of Your New Tattoo*. It had his name and address at the bottom. She read it and nodded. He turned and gave me a card, too.

"Anything for you today?" he asked me.

"No, no. I'm a chaperon, that's all."

"Too bad. You'd tattoo great. You're pale—high contrast." He reached up and tapped me on the collarbone.

Babs looked a little white herself now, standing up, zipping her pants. Tiny got his tie and put it back on, tightened it as we walked around front.

"I like to look natty," he told me. Then he said to Steve, all business, "Eight dollars."

The boys crowded around Babs, who was suddenly looking pleased and jaunty, shaking her head: no, it didn't hurt; no big deal; no, not now, I'll show it to you later. I'm still the only member of the family that knows she has that tattoo.

"You wanna stick around and chat awhile?" Tiny asked me, pocketing Steve's money. "Tuesday's my slow day."

The boys turned and looked at me, like I was the tough one all of a sudden; I could see Babs was jealous.

"Sure," I said.

"Careful, Lois," said Steve. "By the time that character gets through with you, you'll be the tattooed lady."

* * *

But he didn't give me my first tattoo till a year later, the day after we were married: a little butterfly pooled in the small of my back. Five years later, he began referring to it as his "early work," even though he'd been tattooing for twenty-five years before he met me. That didn't rankle me as much as you might think—I liked being his early body of work, work-in-progress, future. That little butterfly sat by itself for a while, but in five years' time Tiny flooded it with other designs: carnations, an apple, a bomber plane, his initials.

When I told my mother about that first tattoo, she said, "Oh Lord. Is it pretty?" Like all good mothers, she always knew the worst was going to happen and was disappointed and relieved when it finally did. But she didn't ask to see that tattoo, or any of the ones that followed. Sunday afternoons, when I went to have lunch with her, I dressed very carefully. I covered myself whenever I left the shop, anyhow: I hated nosy women in the grocery store trying to read my arm as I reached for the peas; I suspected all waitresses of gossiping about me in the kitchen. On my visits to my mother, though, I was extra wary. Through the years, my sleeves got longer, the fabrics more opaque. I never wore white when I visited her: the colors shimmered through.

How could I explain it to my mother? She has always been a glamorous woman, never going anywhere without a mirror, checking and rechecking her reflection, straightening, maintaining. When I was a teenager, there were days that I didn't look in a mirror at all; I avoided my shadow passing in shop windows.

Makeup hated me: mascara blacked my eyes, lipstick found its way onto my teeth and chin. At best, on formal occasions, I would peer into the rectangle on my lipstick case, seeing my mouth and nothing more. Tiny changed that. He caught me kneeling on the bathroom counter trying to get a glimpse of part of my back between the medicine chest and a compact, and he went on a campaign, installing mirrors, hiding them. He put a triple mirror from a clothing shop in our bedroom, put a full-length mirror over the bathtub. Once, I opened the freezer and saw my own reflection, chalked up with frost, looking alarmed in a red plastic frame in front of the orange juice.

Most of Tiny's own tattoos were ancient things that he'd done when he was just starting out. He learned the art traveling with the circus in the thirties, could only practice on himself or a grapefruit, and sometimes there wasn't a grapefruit around. The top of his left thigh was almost solid black with experiments.

When we were first married, he revealed a different tattoo every night, all of them hidden away: one night, a rose on a big toe; next, a banner that said E PLURIBUS UNUM half-furled in the hinge of his armpit; the next, his own signature, crooked and ugly, on the inside of his lip. One night, he said, "Are you ready?" and before I could answer he turned his eyelids inside out, and there was a black star floating on the back of each one, isolated, like a scientific experiment.

"Flipping them up," he said, turning them back, "hurts more than the needle does. I was young and drunk and crazy when I had those done, and the guy who did them was younger and drunker and crazier. I'm lucky he stopped there, didn't tattoo my eyeballs scarlet red."

He showed me all these designs like he was performing magic tricks, and sometimes I expected him to wave his hand over his toe and the rose would disappear and end up cupped in his palm; or the banner would finish rolling out from under his arm straight into the air, and go up in a flash of fire; or his name would unwrite itself; or I would fall asleep and find, in front of my own eyes, those floating stars, as black and unruly as Tiny's hair.

It didn't take me long to get used to the feel of the needle. I learned to love it. Tiny gave me maybe two tattoos a year for our first four years of marriage. Little ones. The bigger ones took form over several months, or even longer. He sometimes did sketches for them on his own knee. I started sitting in the shop in a halter top and high cut, low slung shorts, ready to get up and turn a thigh this way or that, showing the customers how the colors went. I saw the same sorts of people I'd seen Tuesdays before I married Tiny, plus others: businessmen, priests, telephone operators, school-board members. Now they started asking me: "Does it hurt?" I told the truth. Of course it hurts, about the same as a vaccination, a lightly skinned knee, but less than a well-landed punch, a bad muscle cramp, or paying the bills. And look what you get: something that can't be stolen, pawned, lost, forgotten, or outgrown.

In the late sixties, when Tiny was still working on a small scale, every time I got a new tattoo, I'd steal a daily touch—I would feel the scab starting, covering the colors, and I'd get impatient and think about peeling it off myself. Tiny'd read my mind and bawl me out, so I'd just run my finger over the tattoo, feeling the outline raised up like it always is when fresh. Then it'd peel by itself, and one day I'd put my finger down and not be able to tell the difference in skin: it'd really be a part of me. And that's when I started wanting another one.

After we'd been married ten years, Tiny got interested in art. Mother had given me a big book called *Masterpieces of the Renaissance*—she wanted me to latch on to something, to go to college, and she figured art history, all things considered, might appeal to me. It was a beautiful book—the gloss of the paper made all the paintings look just finished; the pages gave off the scent of brand new things. I read it the day I got it, and set it aside. The next afternoon, I picked it up and all the reproductions had been taken out with a razor blade. No Raphael, Michelangelo—just a tunnel of empty frames where they'd been, front of the book to back.

I ran down to the shop, grumbling. The plates from the book were tacked up on the wall; Tiny was eyeing an El Greco and sketching.

"What do you think you're doing?" I asked, hands on my hips, the way my mother stood when she started a fight.

"Take off your pants," he said.

"You ruined my book."

"I saved your mom's inscription. When I'm finished, we'll tape all the pictures back in. Come on, Lois, I want to try something."

"I don't feel like getting tattooed today, thank you very much."

"Pen and ink, that's all. I just want to sketch something."

"Sketch it on paper."

"Paper doesn't curve as nice as you. It'll only take a minute. Please?"

So I gave in, and Tiny sketched something on my hip in ballpoint pen. He didn't like whatever he'd done, and wiped my hip clean with rubbing alcohol. The next day he tried again. He took his time. I got a book to read while he was working (I couldn't get interested in something that wasn't permanent), but I couldn't figure out how to arrange myself. I leaned this way and that, holding my book at arm's length, and Tiny told me to stop squirming. Every night for a week he sketched and erased. At the end of the sessions, my hands would be dead asleep from trying to hold the book steady, and when I hit them on the edge of the table, trying to rouse them, they'd buzz like tuning forks. He never let me see what he was doing.

One night at the end of the week, after closing, Tiny said he had achieved what he wanted. He planned to tattoo it on my hip as a surprise.

I balked; my hip was my own, and I wanted to know what was going to be there. He promised that it would be beautiful and decent and a masterpiece.

"You'll love it," he said. "I've got this painting racket figured out."

"Okay," I said.

He decided to do the work upstairs at home. I stretched out on the bed, and he put on some Bing Crosby. Tiny loved Bing Crosby and at one point wanted to tattoo his face on me, but I put my foot down on that one. He gave me a glass of wine; he often let me have a glass, maybe two, when he was working on me. Never more, because it was against his strictest principles to tattoo a drunk.

He started at eight and worked until eleven. Tiny had a light touch, and by the end of the evening I had a little bit of El Greco. The colors weren't quite right, but it was mostly wonderful, the face of a Spanish monk blooming on my hip: Fray Felix Hortensio Paravacino. Tiny was good, believe it.

He adapted a lot of paintings from that book, did them up in flash and hung them in his shop. Few people asked for those designs—he thought of them mostly as eye-catchers, anyhow—but one skinny lady had the Mona Lisa put on her back, all those folds of fabric, the little winding roads in the background.

"Lucky she's built like a boy," Tiny said, meaning the woman, not Mona Lisa. "Otherwise, the picture woulda been all lopsided."

We went to the Art Center every now and then and wandered through one square room after another. I tried to get Tiny to look at my favorite thing there, a little Van Gogh landscape, but he always shook his head.

"That guy," said Tiny. "He's not a painter, he's a sculptor."

All those paintings and little descriptions made me sleepy; I would sprawl on a bench while Tiny practically pressed his nose to the oldest canvases.

We made the guards very nervous.

Tiny started to work bigger all the time, and put designs on my arms, down my legs. Eventually, he left only my hands, my feet, my neck, and face blank—I can still get dressed and look unmarked. But look at me undressed, see how he got better over the years: his patriotic stage, his religious stage. He liked greens and reds especially, and fine single-needle outlines, which he called "rare and elegant." I've got George Washington on one arm and Lincoln freeing the slaves on the other; I've got a garden planted between my breasts, Japanese peonies and daisies, reds and faded yellows; I've got a little pair of arms sinking into my belly button captioned HELP LET ME OUT.

My life drove my mother crazy. All she wanted was for me to become miraculously blank. I broke her heart—that was my job. She let me know her heart was broken—that was hers. She loved me, loves me. She has had a thousand lives: as a girl, she was pretty and could dance and flirt; her mother died, and she learned to take care of her father and older brother, and still she was happy, poised, and courted. She worked her way through college cleaning houses; she went to law school and New York and had a practice for a while; she married the owner of a women's clothing store and moved to the Midwest; she went to Indianapolis to learn how to fit women's underwear, and has her G.C. (Graduate Corsetiere) from the Gossard School. When my father died in 1955, she took over the shop herself and ran it for twenty years. She has taught ballroom dancing, travels to foreign countries; she is a small-business consultant, the vice-president of her temple, and president of the sisterhood. She used to paint, sculpt, needlepoint, and knit, and there is a table in the front hall of her apartment that she made sixty years ago. My mother believes in being able to start fresh whenever life demands. Tattoos confound her.

One Sunday when I was thirty and just beginning to become the tattooed lady (Tiny had started the Ascension the week before), my mother poured me a cup of coffee and said, "Sweethearts carve their names on trees, not each other. Does it ever occur to you that you are not leading a normal life?"

"Yes," I said. "Thank you." I adjusted my pants and peered at my ankle to see whether I had embarrassed myself, whether a tattoo had managed to come loose and slip to the floor. My cousin Babs, who had just had a baby, was coming to lunch, too, and my mother and I sat on the brocade sofa waiting.

"I just feel that you're painting yourself into a corner," Mom said to me. "How's Tiny?"

"Doing very well," I said. "Business is up." My mother winced.

The doorbell rang. Mom answered the bell and ushered in Babs, still a little thick around the middle, but elegant in her suit, stockings of just the right color, curled hair.

Mom sat her down on the sofa.

"Honey," she said. "How's the darling baby?"

"A baby, all the way," said Babs. "No, he's fine, he's sweet."

"Well," said Mom. "Look at those nice clothes."

Babs had calmed down in the passing years; her parents had offered her a car if she stopped seeing Steve, and it was a better-than-fair deal. After college, she met and married a high school principal turned local politician, and she seemed to have lost every drop of wildness in her.

The sight of a well-dressed Babs never failed to surprise me. "No one would ever suspect you had a reckless youth," I told her.

"It's true," said Babs. She looked at me with some regret and sighed. "Now I'm a nice married lady who sometimes has one too many glasses of whiskey at one of my husband's parties and then tells the truth." She sighed and shifted her weight on the sofa cushion. I imagined her bow tattoo pricking her skin, an old war injury kicking up.

The three of us sat there and chatted about local news, babies, recipes. We covered ourselves. Looking at my mother, I realized how little I knew of her. Recently, I had gone through her desk, trying to unearth a phone book, and found a doctor's bill for a mammogram, detailing two suspicious spots, the next appointment. My heart jumped whenever I thought of it. Did her body show what happened next? Her face didn't, and nobody—especially me—asked my mother such things. Babs, too—besides that bit of color, what else: stretched-out stomach, the zipper of a surgical scar?

I knew myself under my green pantsuit, could tap George Washington on the chin, prick a finger on the thorn of a rose, strum an apocalyptic angel's wing, trace the shape of a heart Tiny'd given me after our first fight.

Anyone could read me like a book.

When my mother took the dirty dishes to the kitchen, I leaned toward Babs.

"Watch that whiskey," I told her, "or sometime you'll drop your pants to show a visiting dignitary the colorful result of a misspent youth."

She looked sad and understanding. "Oh," she whispered, "I *know*."

That night, after Babs left, my mother took me to her bedroom closet to give me some of her old clothing. She was almost as tall as I was and very fashionable, her hand-me-downs nicer than my new things.

"Here," she said, handing me a pile of skirts and dresses. "Try them on. Don't take what you can't use."

I started for the bathroom to change.

She sighed. "I'm your mother," she said. "I used to fit girdles on women with stranger bodies than yours. You don't have to be modest."

So I undressed there and tried on the clothes, and my mother looked at me and frowned. Afterward, I sat down on her bed in my underwear and lit a cigarette.

"Wouldn't you like something to eat?" she asked me.

I did, but couldn't. I had just taken up smoking because I had put on a few pounds, and Tiny told me I better cut it out before I changed the expressions of all the tattoos. If I wasn't careful, Washington and Jesus and Fray Felix would start to look surprised or, at best, nauseated.

"No thanks," I told her.

My mother, who only smoked in airports and hospital waiting rooms ("All that cleanliness and worry gets to me," she'd say), slid a cigarette from my pack, took mine from my hand, and lit the end of hers. She looked at all of me stretched along the bed, started to touch my skin, but took her finger away.

"Well," she said, blowing out smoke, "you've finally made yourself into the freak you always thought you were."

I looked at her sideways, not knowing what to say.

"Actually," she said, "you look a little like a calico cat."

My mother was wrong. I never felt like a freak because of my height: I felt like a ghost haunting too much space, like those parents who talk about rattling around the house when the kids move out. I rattled. It's like when you move into a new place, and despite the lease and despite the rent you've paid, the place doesn't feel like home and you're not sure you want to stay. Maybe you don't unpack for a while, maybe you leave the walls blank and put off filling the refrigerator. Well, getting a tattoo—it's like hanging drapes, or laying carpet, or driving that first nail into the fresh plaster: it's deciding you've moved in.

When Tiny turned seventy, he retired. His hands were beginning to shake a little, and he hated the idea of doing sloppy work. We still had the apartment over the shop, and Tiny kept the store open so that people could come in and talk. Nobody took him up on the tattooing lessons he offered; after a while, he tried to convince me to learn. He said I'd attract a lot of business. I told him no, I didn't have the nerves, I wasn't brave like him.

I took a job at the public library instead, shelving books. I worked in the stacks all day, and when I came home, Tiny'd be asleep. I'd know that he'd been napping all day so that he'd be awake enough to stay up and chat. He was getting old fast, now that he wasn't working.

I pulled the dining room table into the shop's front window, because Tiny liked to see who was coming and going. He knocked on the glass and waved, even to strangers. One night, a week before his seventy-sixth birthday, his arm started hurting halfway through dinner.

"I'm calling an ambulance," I said.

"Don't," he told me. "It's like saying there's something wrong. It's bad luck."

"It's bad luck to die," I said, and phoned.

He was surprisingly solid in that hospital bed, unlike his roommate, who looked like he had withered away to bedding. After a week, that roommate disappeared and was replaced by a huge man, a college professor with a heart problem.

One day, Tiny asked me an impossible favor. He wanted me to bring in the needle and put my initials on him.

"Ah, Tiny," I told him. "I'm not ready to sign you off yet."

"You have my initials on you, but I don't have yours. It's bad luck."

"I don't know how."

"You've seen it a million times."

The college professor was eavesdropping, and he looked a little queasy.

"We'll get caught," I whispered.

"We'll be quiet."

"This is a hospital," I said, like maybe he hadn't noticed.

"Sterile conditions," he answered.

So I brought the needle and some black ink the next day, rolled up my sleeves, got to work. We had to bribe the professor quiet, but he was easily bought. All he wanted was quart bottles of Old Milwaukee and the sort of food that would kill him. We turned on the television set to drown out the needle's hum. The professor pretended to sleep, so that if a nurse came in he could plead innocent.

We lived in terror of those nurses. One of them might walk in on us or notice something new on Tiny's arm. Tiny might die while I was working on him, and the hospital would conclude tattooing was some weird form of euthanasia. The professor might raise his price and demand fancier food, imported beers I couldn't afford.

I started with a *G*, and put an *E* on the next day. That afternoon, when I was just sitting there watching Tiny sleep, he raised his eyelids to half mast and muttered, "I wish I woulda finished you."

"I thought I was finished, Tiny," I said.

"Nope," he said. He put a hand on my arm; his nails were rippled like old wood. "A tree, for instance. You don't have a tree."

"Where's room?"

"Soles of feet, earlobes. There's always room. Too late now. But you'll change anyhow, needle or no. For instance, when I put that George Washington on you, he was frowning. By the time you're my age, he'll be grinning ear to ear." He yawned, then suddenly pulled himself onto his elbows, squeezing the one hand on my arm for support. "I mean, tell me," he said. "Do you feel finished?"

"Yes," I said, and although I was thirty-nine, it was true: it hadn't occurred to me until that minute that I'd have to exist after he was gone.

The next day I was putting a *T* on his arm when Tiny said, "Do me a favor, Lois, huh? Don't forget me?"

The professor began to giggle in bed and ended up laughing, hard. "Do you think she'd be able to, even if she wanted? Look at her—she's a human memo board."

I really thought that I would keep on going, that I'd put a letter a day on him for a year, more. I hoped it would keep him going, because he seemed to be giving up a little.

By the end of the week, Tiny's arm said GET WELL in letters of all different sizes.

"Well," he said. "It's a little boring."

"It's going to get more interesting."

"It better," he told me, smiling. "Tomorrow you can put on a horseshoe for luck. Get fancy. Put on a heart for love."

"Okay," I said. But he died in the night, left without my name or love, with only my good wishes on his arm.

"What's going to happen to you now?" my mother asked me. "What if you want to get married again? What man will want you when someone else has been scribbling all over you?"

A month after Tiny died, Mama told me she was going to start inviting nice young men to our Sunday lunches. She bought me new outfits, unrevealing ones, and told me that we should keep my figure secret—she always referred to it as my figure, as if, over the years, I had put on a few things that could easily be taken off. I go to keep her happy, and sit on one side of the sofa while the fat divorced sons of her friends flirt with her instead of me, knowing that'll get them further. Sometimes I eat fudge and don't say one word all afternoon.

Every day I get up and go to work at the library, dressed in short skirts, short sleeves, no stockings. The director has told me that I'm frightening people.

"I'm sorry," I told her. "These are my widow's weeds."

Three weeks ago I got a letter from a young man on the coast, a tattooist who said that Tiny was a great artist and that I was proof of it. He wanted to take my photo, see the whole gallery. I packed him a box of Tiny's things, old flash sheets and needles and pages of El Greco, and told him to study those. He called me and said I was better than any museum. I told him that I apologized, that I understood, but really: I am not a museum, not yet, I'm a love letter, a love letter.

SOME HAVE ENTERTAINED ANGELS, UNAWARE

I

MY PARENTS WERE NOT handy people. They understood nothing of plumbing, were mystified by the laying of linoleum, followed electrical lines terrified of what was at the other end. Our Victorian was cheap because it needed so much work: the stained-glass windows held only a few colored panes between their crossed fingers; the wood doors between the dining room and living room had to be threatened before they'd slide open. When I was very small, the house seemed always about to explode. Sometimes it did, in a minor way: a flood in the basement, a fire in the chimney, the birth of my brother, Jackie. When my mother died of a cerebral hemorrhage—I was six and Jackie three—Dad explained it this way: bad plumbing, faulty wiring. Beyond repair.

Two months later, Dad started to take in strays, mostly the human sort: drunks, debtors, divorcées, deadbeats. He had a strange admiration for people unable to earn a living, gave the strangers he met in bars musty bedrooms we never even went into. The strangers began to fix things. They started with their own rooms, then crept through the house, ripping up and nailing down. Bobby Noonan, a forty-year-old flute player who refused what he thought of as demeaning gigs—under a roof, say, or for a definite fee—knew how to make a hot-water faucet live up to its promise, and handled people as smoothly. It was Bobby, smoking a pipe, who directed the poet with the waist-length hair and Fu Manchu mustache to clamber onto the roof and reshingle; it was Bobby who kept the elderly lady painter away from the paint buckets, knowing she was frequently inspired to pornographic murals. For a while Dad walked around the house, stopping to steady a ladder, hold nails in his hand. He hummed, a fond half smile on his face. Things, it could not be denied, were getting done. Mike Ianelli, the poet, worked wood into furniture and bookshelves; Gertrude, our muralist, was, at sixty-five, a startlingly good welder. I still remember the joy of discovering that the upstairs bathroom had an actual door and, what was more amazing, a toilet you could flush and flush.

Our house grew thick with people. In the kitchen, Suzanne Peterson, pale and bitter as aspirin, stirred the dimpled pots that held our meals. Kenneth Graves, graduate student forever, meditated on the dining room table twice a day and even so was nervous enough to threaten to kill a passing Avon lady. Bobby considered him delicate, and gave him baby-sitting duty.

Jackie and I were moved to new bedrooms in the recently refurbished attic. Mine was papered with flowers and had doll furniture Mike had made from scraps of old wood. Jackie's room was blue, with a stark rocking horse that had a mop for a mane and a marble for its one eye—Mike again. For the first month, I slept badly: sometime before, a screech owl had flown under the eaves, and all I could remember was the flapping and Dad's swearing. Jackie says now that Dad gave our real rooms away and banished us. But our beds were quiet and safe; only trees paced over our ceilings. I forgot the screech owl soon enough and slept better than I ever have since, there beneath the clasped hands of the roof.

Some boarders stayed for years; others came and went quickly. Every night for a month, a fat young man named Candy cried himself to sleep in his room. Denny Horkan moved his lumpy Irish body into the corners of the house for seven weeks, leaving behind first religious tracts and then pointed personal notes ("Your on the road to hell," the last one said. "Guess its just as well"). A man whose name we never knew—we called him Mr. Nobody—moved in and out the same day, taking with him Suzanne's extensive spice rack. Dad considered the dullards his only mistakes. He pictured Mr. Nobody in a seedy hotel room downtown, rubbing his hands and bald head, surrounded by thin twigs of saffron, insolent cumin, whispering, "Lovely; sweet." He imagined Denny Horkan at the gates of heaven, explaining that he tried, he tried, but there were so many sinners, and so stubborn. When a room emptied, Dad sat at the kitchen table and invented boarders for it, gave them wooden legs, trunks rattling with butterfly collections and murdered wives.

Photographs started to clutter the mantelpiece: Jackie and Bobby at Halloween, candles beneath their chins; Jackie, at four, rushing through Cabot Woods on Mike's shoulders; me, at seven, on Kenneth Graves's lap in the heat of summer, both of us too skinny, elbows and knees our roundest parts, looking as if nothing could save us.

Dad hated those people so inconsiderate as to move in, move out, never making a noise, a scene, a mark, a complaint. A good story when you left was the only rent he insisted on.

For instance: one day at 5 A.M., a figure packed a grip, stole out the front door, and got almost all the way down the porch stairs before falling, sending clothing and bottles flying. The house woke up, one dark window at a time, and watched the fugitive pile damp shattered things into the open suitcase, then limp away, dripping cable-knit sweaters, whiskey, cusswords. The next morning we found a check for five thousand dollars on the kitchen table and half a tooth on the front walk.

That figure was my father.

Need more information? Dad was a librarian; he'd tell you: cross-reference. The books in his bedroom did that for you. If you looked in one, it sent you to another, which was an index to a third, which led you to a four-volume set, a yearbook, a bibliography. Even when you thought you were closing in, the last book spun you in circles inside itself: see this footnote, that article.

My father, who had no references, was just as dizzying. He himself said that facts could always be tracked down. Find the Latin root: conjugate, decline.

My father conjugated: go, going, lost.

* * *

My first memory takes place somewhere dark, with light the color of honey, and as sticky. I sit low to the ground—on a curb?—and listen to a dozen voices, themselves like honey, thick and unfathomably sweet. One of my father's dusty shoes is parked beside me, and I tie and untie it. After a while my fingers ache with the effort.

A few years later, I realized: I was on the footrail of the Kinvaraugh pub, listening to my father get drunk.

Before the boarders came, the bars were Dad's best babysitters. At three and six, Jackie and I frequented the Black Rose, the Plough and the Stars, George's, the Silhouette. Dad took us on his days off when the barkeeps wouldn't mind, Sundays when we could spin on the stools or sit right on the bar, taking occasional sips of ale from the big-mouthed glasses offered to us. Jackie liked the taste so much that *beer* was one of his first words. The only time Dad's mother, a teetotaler, visited us, Jackie responded to the mid-morning crack of a can by yelling the word, loud; he rushed to the kitchen, revealing Dad in the pantry, trying to hide a fresh case of Miller behind his slim hips.

Of course, if you tell this story in front of Jackie now, he insists it never happened.

Dad was thin then—maybe still is—and as chinless and gloomy as a clarinet. His voice was low and musical, trilled by a stutter; it squealed with air when he was upset. My mother was as squat and brassy as Dad was narrow and reedy; the one thing I remember her saying is, "For God's sake, Peter, talk like a grown man."

Dad was a good librarian, obsessed with things other people never thought of. He loved obscure comedians of the twenties and thirties, put their pictures up in his room, watched their brittle black-and-white movies on the wall as they rattled through his projector. His favorite was a burlesque team that had one member who wore greasepaint glasses drawn right on his face. They had a good story: after falling out of fame, the fellow without the glasses got depressed and was committed to a sanatorium. Two years later, he seemed better, and his partner—who was doing well as a single—came to pick him up. In the car, the asylum insignificant in the rearview mirror, they fantasized about a comeback: the halls they would play, new movies, new fame. Maybe they even believed it. Suddenly, the depressed man pointed to the slick stripes of a barber's pole and asked his partner to stop: he wanted an old-fashioned shave, a pampering. Probably, his friend made a joke—surely after two years it would be nice to hold a sharp object in your hand—but pulled up to the curb anyhow. Inside the shop, just after the barber had lathered the pink peak of chin, the man jumped up and with one gesture grabbed the razor and slit his own throat from side to side.

This was Dad's favorite bedtime story.

And that's all I have of my father: spools of film featuring the long dead, and facts from other people's lives. Dad handed out bits of biography the way most folks slip children candy or loose change. He kept a supply: the life of Louis Wain, mad English cat painter; the death toll of the Great Boston Molasses Flood; the way St. Catherine of Siena once caught the severed head of a sinner who, as is usual, found God seconds before the ax struck his neck, the blow so hard it jugged his ears.

Dad kept his stories more and more to himself the longer the boarders stayed, the more work they got done. He rarely went into the rooms as they were fixed, and instead stuck to those he had always used: the kitchen, the downstairs bath, his bedroom. One late evening the boarders managed to talk him into the front parlor for a visit. Bobby told stories of his youth in South Boston, full of brogues and snatches of lullabies. Mike, our long-haired poet, jumped up and acted out some childhood crisis, speaking the parts of his fat Italian papa, his full-blooded Cherokee mother, and one sister who, inexplicably, was part Samoan. Other boarders told their stories. Finally, at a lull, Mike said to Dad, "Your turn, Pete."

Dad cleared his throat. "One day, young John Stuart Mill said to his father . . ."

"No," Mike said. "A story about your own family."

"There aren't any," said Dad.

"Sure there are."

"Really," Dad said. "I don't remember."

"Any story," Bobby said. "We're interested."

"Look," said Dad, madder than I'd ever seen him before. "I don't own any, okay? The family tree—" he took a deep breath, "—begins with me."

Knowing that he'd never leave anything unresearched, I'm sure that he climbed that tree and found nothing: honest lawyers, old age, paid debts. I met his mother that one time, and she was the only relative I ever saw. His parents, I suspect, were dull, habitual churchgoers who never did anything of note and might still live somewhere in Connecticut. Dad had to make do with hand-me-downs from people in books: the roguish, the doomed-from-birth, the boisterous and misused. He wanted his children to have better. That's why he took in the boarders; that's why he left. Jackie says that I give Dad too much credit, that the truth of the matter is Dad had no control over our peculiar childhood. I say that each explosion, each unfamiliar man gargling in our bathroom, was a present to help us get along with strangers in bars. Jackie doesn't drink. I am firm in my belief.

Because really, what other explanation is there? Dad never seemed to like any of those bodies buzzing through the house. He only sat at the kitchen table when everybody was gone or when someone was pouring good whiskey or cheap beer. Mornings, he stood up at the kitchen counter, watching his cigarette burn in the ashtray.

One morning Mike had an especially wicked hangover. He watched Candy, our weeper, who as usual was absurdly cheerful at breakfast. Candy poured sugar over everything, including bacon, humming to himself. I was eating instant oatmeal, which I had made myself with water from the tap. Mike put his hand on my shoulder and pointed at Candy's plate.

"Look at that," he whispered.

I loved Mike best of all the boarders—he had beautiful blue eyes—so to be agreeable, I said, "Bleah," as loudly as possible.

"Disgusting, isn't it, Annie," Mike said.

"Cut your hair," said Candy, as if it were a compliment. "That's even more disgusting."

"My hair matches my mustache perfectly," said Mike. "Besides, I'm not going to die of hair. But that stuff'll kill you."

"Michael," said Candy, and you could hear his good mood leaving him, "could we not talk about death first thing in the morning?"

"I just don't want this lovely child to think that's a normal way to eat."

Candy put his fork down and stood to face Mike, smiling nervously. "Listen—"

"Are you looking for a fight?" Mike asked.

Even I could tell it was a joke, but Candy's big eyes got even bigger. He was made up entirely of circles, the way they teach you to draw cartoons from a book: round head, belly, haircut, knees, and a little round sailor's knot of a nose with no bridge whatsoever. I couldn't imagine how his glasses stayed up. He was trying to make himself look taller and tougher now, and only made himself seem even rounder. "Listen, Mike—"

"Forget it, Chubs," said Mike. "Eat what you want."

Candy turned to face my father, who still stood at the counter. "Pete," said Candy. "Make Mike stop."

My father, who hadn't been paying attention, looked up from his coffee. Finally, he said, "Fend for yourself. I'm not your father. Do I look like I'm in charge?" He waved his hand around the kitchen. "Does any of this look like it belongs to me?"

And it's true, my father rarely said, this is mine. He claimed very little: not stories, not furniture, not children. He wore bow ties because they reminded him of famous people who wore bow ties; he always wanted to name our pets after famous animals in literature.

"But they're ours," Jackie and I would say.

Not long before Dad left, he, Jackie, and I sat in the kitchen. Jackie and I were doing a huge jigsaw puzzle; Dad sat across from us, trying to figure out where to set down his beer.

Suzanne came in wearing a dress that I immediately recognized as belonging to my mother. Suzanne was skinny; the waist hung down to her hips.

"I found this in the downstairs closet," she said. "Do you think I could keep it?"

She turned a little; I could smell my mother coming off the fabric in waves.

"By all means," my father said after a minute. "It belonged to someone who used to live here."

Two days later, Bobby, our flute player, had to ask Dad to please stop fixing things. My father, despite the people with skilled hands and know-how, still installed phones that bounced off the walls on the first ring and had caulked the bathroom so indiscriminately, and with such enthusiasm, that all that was needed was a little bride and groom up by the shower head. Didn't he realize, Bobby asked him, that he was beginning to break working things instead of merely making already-broken things worse? Dad was a mind person, said Bobby, and should concentrate on the living things, of which there were plenty.

This was the November I was eleven, and there was not only Candy weeping in his room, but Lucky, an affable and doomed retriever with a rare appetite that had already claimed two neighborhood kittens, a sprinkler system, and an elderly poodle named Queen Marie. Also Anastasia, a Russian wolfhound, who lounged on the fainting couch all day, displaying, according to Mike, all ten of Ann Landers's Signs that Your Child Is on Drugs; Kenneth Graves's three finches, Sidney, Sidney, and Sidney-Lou; Gert's cat, Tommy, a genius, she said, who, having learned to ride on her shoulders, had taken to leaping off the fridge onto any passing head. There were Suzanne's potted palms; avocado pits sprouting in the windowsills; a few gangly, uninvited spiders; and two sad and witty children who seemed pretty well taken care of by everybody but their father. You could almost see Dad in the front hall, turning slowly, surrounded by living things, knowing that he could fix none of them.

II

"YOU CAN'T BLAME HIM," BOBBY SAID THE MORNING DAD LEFT, feeling personally responsible.

Kenneth Graves disagreed with Bobby and said that he could blame Dad, absolutely. Kenneth Graves had a talent for blame.

Jackie and I sat at the kitchen table, not quite knowing what the fuss was about, listening to Suzanne and the bacon curse at each other. Gertrude clonked in, dressed as usual—patterned capris splattered with paint and a puffy-sleeved sweater with beads in the knit. Old as she was (and she seemed very old to me then), she was skinny as a twelve-year-old. Most mornings, she was the first one awake in the house. Today, she looked around and said, "Good morning, Sunshine! This is more like it."

Mike, pulling himself onto the counter, said, "The master of the castle has deserted." He brushed English muffin crumbs out of his mustache.

"Oh good," said Gert. "Let's have a party."

Suzanne was least cheerful. She got along well with Dad, was formal and polite to Bobby, barely tolerated Mike, ignored Gert, and hated Kenneth Graves with an intensity that I only realized years later comes of having slept with a person.

"Well?" she said.

"Well," said Bobby. He shrugged, looking like the sort of father a lonely child might invent, with his thick, already white hair and the swell of a pipe in a back pocket. Being the cleanest person in the room, he was tacitly put in charge. "So," he said to Jackie and me. "It looks like your father's gone for a while. But we plan to stick around and take care of you guys."

Suzanne smacked a fork onto the counter.

"Because," said Bobby, "he asked us to."

"He did not," Suzanne said. "He left us a check."

Bobby crossed his long legs underneath the kitchen table, bumping one knee. He tugged at the ripples in his ironed blue jeans. "It says *children* on the memo line."

Then, in his first official act as unofficial head of the household, he asked Suzanne, the only boarder with a driver's license, to take the two of us to school. It was a difficult job—the seat of my father's old Cadillac had broken, and he had propped it up with a box full of empty beer bottles. Suzanne sullenly balanced on the edge and nearly ran down the crossing guard.

That night, a group of Dad's friends from his job at the library came over. They were all odd women, the sorts of things that would result from a high school Woman Making 101 class: legs of unequal lengths, eyes crossed, noses too big or too small for their settings, women no wider from hip to hip than from ear to ear. There were at least a half dozen of them, all talking at once: he had just quit the day before, no notice. What was wrong? No tragedy, they hoped? They loved him, they assured us, like a son. Where was Petey, anyhow?

Jackie and Bobby and I sat on the sofa, unable to speak. No thank you, said the ladies, they wouldn't sit down, they really had to be going. They just wanted to bring the things Petey had left behind in his locker: a necktie, a comb (one lady pulled the objects from a shopping bag; the others identified the things aloud), a book on the Swedish royal family, last year's *Guiness*

Book of World Records, some cancelled checks, and three letters containing the words *failure to pay will result in the following.* The leader of the group, the thinnest, oddest of them all, gave us a care package that included a bunch of bananas one step away from compost and a plastic bag of rolls branded with a sticker that said REDUCED FOR QUICK SALE.

When they fluttered out, the leader lingered a minute. Instead of saying goodnight, she whispered, "God give us strength."

Gone, gone; we heard the words all day long. "Well," Bobby told us after the library ladies had left, "he quit his job. Looks like he's really gone."

That night, Jackie came into my room, saying he was scared. He was wearing a set of flowered thermal underwear several sizes too big; I decided, looking at them, that they were probably mine, although in our house there were always pieces of mystery clothing.

"Don't worry," I told him. "I'm sure Daddy will be back." This was a lie. I felt pretty grown-up, being able to tell comforting falsehoods to a child.

"No," he said. He bit his lip. "Those ladies."

I understood in an instant. Dad's room was empty now, and we'd begin to look for a body to put in it. Is that why the women came to visit? Were they looking around? It wasn't their strangeness, their telegraphic words that scared Jackie: it was those bananas. Our boarders always brought us food. Suzanne got leftovers from her catering jobs: crackers damp with parsleyed cheese, thin slices of greasy beef, cream puffs shaped like swans with only the heads missing. Kenneth Graves clerked at a health food store downtown, but could bear to steal only bulgur wheat. Mike called him the Bulgarian, and had told him that bulgur wheat was very nice—you had to be careful about insulting Kenneth—but that vegetables were also nice, as were eggs and milk. But the next week it was bulgur again, brown as the bag that carried it. Bobby was the most generous: after a successful night of busking on the Common, he'd walk into the room seriously, shake his head, trying to look poverty-stricken. Then he'd pull out a package from underneath his mackintosh, and inside there'd be a cut-up chicken, pork chops cuddled together, or, on the best nights, steaks for everyone, sparkling like jewels in the white paper.

Jackie and I slept together in my bed that first night of no Dad, curled up close to the slant of the attic, dreaming of half-priced baked goods in plastic: the way they lost their moisture, dwindled, fogged the bag.

The next day, Jackie mentioned his fears to Bobby, who said no, no: that was Dad's bedroom; this was Dad's house. Nobody would move in.

That didn't make much sense to me, and sometimes I thought of our house as a dying patient, that open space waiting for a transplant.

Saturday afternoon, Bobby took us busking—playing music in the park. We'd gone with him a few times before, in the Cadillac. Dad, whose stutter really showed itself in song, was always put in the background; but the lead singers knocked back brandy from collapsible cups steadily between songs and, by the end of the evening, forgot the words. Dad's voice—"G-G-Goodnight, laaaadies!"—rang out over the leads, one of them hesitantly bidding adieu to the ladies, the other, confident, to Irene. My father remembered the words to hundreds of folk songs, even when drunk, although what he sang at home, to a late-night glass of Irish whiskey, was "Besame Mucho."

This time, Bobby, Mike, Gert, Jackie, and I hopped the express bus into town. The singers stayed pretty much sober, taking only sips from a flask to keep warm. Mike and I waltzed in front of the musicians, both of us admirable, knock-kneed failures. The wind pinked our cheeks. Fresh from the first rush of the season, Christmas shoppers stopped to watch us on the way to the subway, and the tweed cap that Jackie passed buckled with coins and bills. Gert, fingered by both whiskey and weather, was bright red by dusk.

We brought home lamb chops from the overpriced butcher's down the street. Suzanne, who was just taking an immense meatloaf from the oven, sulked until Bobby showed her the chops and won over her cook's heart. It was the only time I ever saw him do anything like flirt. Dinner lasted for hours, full of stories of the best meals each person had ever had, the most amazing concerts heard, the most beautiful face encountered. Afterward, Suzanne presented an apple pie as swollen as a bowler hat. She almost cheerfully circled the table, dropping spoonfuls of whipped cream on everybody's slice. Gert, the whiskey pulling at her eyelids, retired to her room. Bottles appeared from cupboards, and Bobby poured cocoa for Jackie and me and himself.

It wasn't an unusual scene in the house, the drinkers and the honorary drinkers around the table, arguing about art. My father was barely missed; unaccustomed to conversation, he had always lapsed into silence or lecture. Nothing new happened. Mike decided, as he did every week, that he wanted to hear "Love and Breakfast," his favorite song. It was the only cut he listened to off an album by an L.A. band called Bootless; Mike had written the words himself. Suzanne and Kenneth took up their usual argument about music: she listened to ancient, rambunctious vocalists, Wagner and Gregorian chants; he could tolerate anything but. The fight always finished for the night at the same point, with one of them playing a song to prove the other's pigheadedness. Tonight, it was Kenneth's turn, and he stood by the record player, one hand on top of the speaker, the other waving Jerry Lee Lewis's voice into the room as if it were smoke. He said, "See? See?"

At eleven o'clock, Bobby looked at us. I was building a cathedral out of the gothic bones; Jackie slept, his arms stretched out on the table, looking like he was trying to evolve out of an amphibious state.

"Okay," Bobby said. "Bedtime. Chop chop."

This was new. Dad let us go to bed whenever we wanted to; he was a firm believer in letting children act on their stupidity until they learned better. For me this threatened to be in the twenty-first century. Bobby woke Jackie and picked him up; Mike led me by the hand and we climbed the stairs to the bathroom. He lay down in the bathtub while Bobby perched on the edge, supervising the brushing of teeth, the scrubbing of faces. Upstairs in our rooms, Bobby found our pajamas and instructed us to put them on. More nights than not, I fell asleep in my clothing. He tucked us into bed firmly, as if the blankets would protect us from sudden shocks.

In the morning, happy to be pajamad, the covers still around him, Jackie suggested that maybe he didn't much miss Dad.

I did, though. I practiced by sitting in his chair in the kitchen, inventing possible lives for him, just as he had for other missing persons. All I could come up with was a clear picture of my father in another kitchen, inventing lives for us.

Bobby announced new rules, among them, regular baths. This was not an issue for Jackie, whose only real quirk was a need to shower at least twice a day, but I had to be coaxed. The job fell to Suzanne. She started with remarks about my personal odor, moved on to threats from my invisible father, and ended with horror stories of mold, small animals, and trees that would take me over: result, the explosion of my insides, a loveless life.

Insulted, I called her the worst thing I could think of, which happened to be something I'd picked up from a fight between Kenneth and her.

"Sure," I said, "you cunty old cow."

She immediately picked me up—I was small for my age, but no baby—tucked me under her arm and climbed the stairs. Certain that she planned to kill me, I decided to behave and maybe win her over. She opened the door to Mike's room and heaved me in. He was sitting cross-legged by the pillows, reading a book. My head landed between his feet.

"If you're so smart," Suzanne yelled at him, "if you're so in charge, you take care of this. She's filthy enough to be your job."

Mike looked at me upside down, raised one eyebrow, then the other. "Don't know what you did, kid," he said, "but I bet you done good." He shook my hand solemnly.

And so I was delivered to Mike. At twenty-three, he was the youngest of our boarders by a couple of years and, in some ways, the flightiest. Kenneth Graves could be counted on for his quotidian oddness, but Mike sometimes disappeared for a week at a time, off on what he called "a bender." On his return, smelling of beer and women, gambling and cigars, he danced a little around the house, touching my hair, Jackie's, saying, "Ah children, ah houseplants, ah purity." The wild red hair, the mustache that he groomed at the breakfast table, told nothing of his real self: He was a tough, sweet guy from Brooklyn who drank bourbon, read Poe, Whitman, and Raymond Chandler. I always thought that a fedora and a suit with razor lapels would suit him better; as it was, he favored overalls and faded T-shirts, and his words—sly, sharp, nasal—slid out from underneath the fringe of his mustache.

Jackie and I agree on this: after Dad left, I was brought up by Mike; he, by Bobby.

"It could've worked out the other way around," says Jackie. "Maybe things would've evened out; we'd be more alike."

"Half crazy, half organized?" I ask.

"Sure."

Never. I love Bobby, still do, but found him distant, rigid. Men of principles have never been my favorite sort. Bobby would have combed my hair daily, he would have turned my sweaters right side out, he would have put me through the whole course of manners that, ever since my airborne arc into Mike's room, I have sorely needed. Mike, given Jackie, would have tried to inject him with poetry, the ability to shoot baskets. These lessons, for me, for Jackie, would never have taken. Mike's handshake was utterly serious. It meant: you may behave as badly as you like. Just relax when you get thrown.

Suzanne gave up cooking. She volunteered to clean, but she

wanted, under no circumstances, to be anyone's mother figure. This she said to Kenneth Graves, who was asleep on the sofa. Bobby and Mike took over in the kitchen, like one of Dad's comedy teams, two men inexplicably together. Bobby specialized in casseroles involving leftovers; he was a little unsure of how to come up with meals of origin. Mike set the table and washed plates. As Bobby stirred the mysterious food, Mike peered over his shoulders—an effort, since Bobby, at six feet two inches, was almost a foot taller—and said, "St. Noonan and the Miracle of the Stewing Meat." Bobby was a Catholic; Mike, who'd been brought up that way, couldn't fathom sticking with it. Mike was right: face blushing from steam, his apron spattered with sauce, Bobby looked no less than saintly. "Please," he murmured, "call me St. Bob."

"St. Noonan and the Resurrection of the Turkey Carcass," answered Mike. "St. Noonan and the Conversion of Last Week's Pot Roast." Once, as Mike had his mouth open to say something, Bobby, not looking around, smacked him on the ear with a ladle and said, "St. Noonan Smites the Infidel."

Two men, two kids—for a while, it was on your marks, get set, go. Whose child would be best adjusted, most charming, most likely to be invited to the White House as either guest or occupant? Mike's kid was older, but Bobby had the head start: Jackie was already his miniature—studious, wanting explanations, not doing things that needed to be explained. Bobby bought him a telescope, and the two of them stuck it out an attic window and peered through it together for hours, hoping for undiscovered comets, for a shy galaxy to drop its robe like an unaware bather in a lit-up window. Afterward, the two of them polished shoes in the kitchen, buffing wingtips, the black polish winking out of the broguing, stars revealing themselves there, in their hands.

We got envelopes from Dad all this time, always with a money order for Bobby and a postcard for Jackie and me. The cards said things like, "The poet Hart Crane jumped off a ship in his pajamas and drowned. His father invented Lifesavers. The candy, not the flotation device." Or, "Dutch Schultz, the Needle Beer King of New Jersey, babbled nonsense for two hours before he died, all of it taken down by a police stenographer. His very last words were, 'French-Canadian Bean Soup.' " Jackie refused to read the cards. I put them up on my walls, writing side out. My father's penmanship was thin and slightly slanted, like he was. Only the postmarks were ugly: no seals from Istanbul, Kalamazoo. Always Cambridge.

He gave us no return address, and lost out on the new stories. They might not have been to his taste. For instance, nobody died. Not in the house, anyhow. Kenneth Graves locked himself in Suzanne's room one day and went through heroin withdrawal, which involved breaking her records, one by one. We felt a little like the man whose wife neglected to mention that she was pregnant before giving birth in the bathtub; nobody, except possibly Suzanne, realized that he was an addict. We had to call the police, who jimmied the lock and dragged him out, swearing and filthy, looking as if he'd grown a full beard since the day before.

He kicked the stuff for good in a government house and moved to New York to escape, as he said, the bad influences around Boston. We got cards from him that said, "Seven weeks and still clean," or, "Three months and no looking back." Two days after we received the Christmas card that said, "Almost a year and going strong," a friend of his called to say that Kenneth Graves had died of an overdose.

"Curiosity," the friend told Mike. "Nostalgia. A one-time-only opportunity. You know how it is."

No family could be tracked down; our house was listed in his address book under *Home*.

That night, we sadly discovered that none of us could think of any really happy memories of him. Suzanne moved out a month later to marry a man we had never met. We thought that was suspicious.

Somehow, Mike and Bobby saw us through the crises of childhood. Jackie, as far as I remember, had exactly one: he stepped out of the tub in the downstairs bathroom and fell, up to his right hip, through the floor, stopping when his foot hit a pipe. Stark naked, unable to reach a towel, acutely embarrassed, he stayed there until Gert opened the door, tilted her head, and said, "Now, there's a scene that ought to be painted." In a tired rage, Jackie threw a bar of soap over her head, then asked her to please get Bobby. He had broken his foot, and it doubled in size beneath the floor. Mike cut a wide hole around the leg while Bobby stood in the bathtub, supporting Jackie by the armpits.

I kept Mike pretty busy. I started by splitting my pants in math class, revealing to the entire fifth grade that, unable to find underwear that morning, I had gone without—the office sent me home with my jacket tied around my waist. The next year, I sprung into school in a pair of pilled-up tights, one of Bobby's turtlenecks, and a wig, announcing that I was the new girl. In junior high school, I tie-dyed the science teacher's lab coat; intimated that the fat gymnastics coach could not do a cartwheel to save her life; was kicked out of Social Studies for making unpleasant remarks about the Crusades. Searching for new stories, I hung around the tough kids for a while. They were bad but uninspired—they stole liquor from their parents, drank steadily until a few delicate girls threw up, and continued until everyone in the room was passed out or weeping.

Mike decided that his job was to teach me how to make trouble without landing in it. Together, we attended Sunday brunch at the Krishna temple and sang the "Hokey Pokey" during the loud prayers, then harassed hapless men dressed in saffron about the nature of life. He took me to tea at the Ritz and announced that it was essential for me to go into the ladies' room, stand on the toilet, and steal crystals from the chandeliers. I did. My junior year in high school, we spent several afternoons in the balcony of a revival movie house in Cambridge smoking pot.

He helped me with my schoolwork, too. On those nights, several times a semester, when I'd walk into the kitchen at seven o'clock and remark that I had a paper due the next day, he'd whisk me away to the Howard Johnson's over the turnpike. We'd drink coffee from the thermos pot all night long—toward morning, Mike would drink right from the spout—and hash out the details.

"Okay," Mike said. "What's the subject?"

I told him, and he lectured awhile, and we made up facts for the paper and books for the bibliography. My father would have been scandalized, but the teachers rarely noticed. They told me to type instead of print or complained about jelly stains or said I should be more focused. I usually got B's on those papers; they were "creative," "lively," "energetic." I only failed one: Mike had convinced me to write a paper on Lefty Frizzell, the country singer, and then proceeded to sing all night long. I got only one sentence out of him: "Intelligent people realize that Lefty Frizzell is synonymous with heartbreak." The teacher failed me because she noticed that one of the books I cited was edited by me and translated by Howard Johnson.

Mike insisted on looking at the papers when I got them back, and swore at the teachers under his breath. He'd hand them to me, muttering, "What do they know."

Mike taught me how to be fearless; Jackie had nothing to fear. He inherited Dad's need to constantly know a new thing, but turned it toward physics, biology. Not even the bullies bothered him. He grew up broad-shouldered, like Bobby, as if he'd acquired those genes by transference, cross-pollination.

Honestly, it never occurred to me, not until recently, that Mike and Bobby might have had something better to do. They seemed happy: they hung around, didn't they? Bobby invited his musician friends to the house—thin red-haired women like matchsticks, men with pewter belt buckles sinking into their soft bellies. A whole series of skinny girls snuck in and out of Mike's room. One even found the kitchen and burned something resembling breakfast until Bobby came and gently took the spatula from her hand, sending her back to Mike.

Gert was the only other regular still puttering around the house. Bobby had insisted on not replacing boarders as they moved out over the years, developing a sudden concern for strangers traipsing through our rooms, forgetting that was how he had become ours. Gert was getting older and vaguer; her paintings got more obscene and specific. You could pose for her fully clothed, ankles crossed, a bouquet of flowers and a serious expression, and she would return you stark naked, knees in opposite corners of the frame, your tongue lolling one way and your eyes another—she charted every hair and gland as carefully as a medieval cartographer, guessing badly. She didn't understand why people weren't willing to sit for her or why, if they did, they declined to look at the results. My senior year in high school, she moved to a retirement home in Florida to "paint on the beach." Dad would have loved to hear that one.

"So you're an orphan," my friend Jenny said to me our junior year in high school. We sat in the kitchen, drunk enough on sweet wine that the late afternoon sun thrilled and amazed us. "No," I said. "It's my mother who's dead. My father's still around."

"Oh." Her parents were divorced, and she thought she understood.

"Cambridge, somewhere," I told her. "We get postcards."

"So he just left?"

"Yup." I poured the last of my wine into my mouth. Mike had taught me to be cavalier about such things.

"Why?"

"Who knows? I mean, my father has his own problems." This was something that Bobby said to us often, usually when he got a check that said my father would not be back, not soon: your father has his own problems.

"It was just time for him to leave," I told Jenny.

And I believed it, I did. People were always moving out of the house. Why should my father outstay his welcome? What was so special about him? Sometimes when I missed him, I imagined that, by the time he left, I'd had about enough of him, that everyone, including me and Jackie, had been secretly hoping for weeks that he would go.

One evening, Mike told the story about the man who couldn't ever remember to fill his gas tank. "We got calls from him all the time," said Mike. "Stranded at the mouth of the turnpike at rush hour; in the middle of downtown Waltham. He was mad as hell whenever he came home, but he always claimed that the average American ran out of gas three times a year, and when he did it that often we could make fun of him, but not until then. Christ, he must have done it that often."

"That was Dad," said Jackie, who never forgot anything.

"Of course. It was Pete." Mike rubbed his head in embarrassment.

Slowly, we filed Dad between Candy and Mr. Nobody: someone who used to live here.

It still makes sense to me. If you're unhappy, you leave. Maybe if I'd known my mother, she'd tell me that people have to compromise. My friends, motherly and helpful, still explain this. They mean men, of course; but I find it hard enough to compromise with the facts of living: a need for vitamins, the ringing telephone. Life yells: accept me, take care of this, you're not paying attention. Compromise with a *person*? Out of the question.

Only love or loneliness can change the part of a man's hair. The following June, a pale path appeared in the center of Mike's head. It was love. He let his new girl braid his hair, too—a fat rope down the back, or twin cords by each ear. Bobby started calling him Pocahontas.

"Shut up, white man," Mike answered peevishly.

" 'By the shores of Gitchee Gumee, by the bright and shining waters—' "

"Okay, okay," said Mike.

After a while, Bobby didn't even have to make an Indian reference; he'd just quote in the right cadence: "Mich-ael will you set the table, pour the water, mix the biscuits."

I had been looking forward to a useless summer palling around with Mike—he was old enough that when we went into bars, I wasn't carded. But Mike had other plans. His new girl looked like the old girls. For all I knew, he was working through one large family.

I moped around the house. Having attended exactly four gym classes in three years, I received an empty tube at graduation. Bobby suggested summer school; Mike promised me that if I wanted, he could get me into college, diploma or no, money or no. This made me nervous. It's true that Mike could talk his way into almost anything, rarely paying for movies or plays. His ruses, however, generally depended on a friend who had taken an overdose and had gone into the theater to die, having spent all the happy moments of his life there.

"Just let me go in and walk him out," Mike told the managers. "I won't make a fuss, I promise. Just give us a little dignity."

I pictured Mike somehow talking the two of us into college. We'd sit in a Poli Sci lecture, and the campus police would burst in, pointing at us. "THERE THEY ARE." We'd escape wildly, jumping off the backs of chairs, other people's heads, then disguise ourselves as Pakistani chemistry students and duck into a lab until we were found again.

Instead, I got a job dispatching for Boston University's buildings-and-grounds department. After a year, I was eligible to take classes free; after another year, I took them up on the offer. I started with a night course on archaeology, and one day, while I was reading a magazine, I found this article.

A colossus once stood in an Eastern country. It was built before written language, but later documents tell us that there have never been words to describe it, never will be. After years in the heat, the marble muscles tired and let go of the features: an ear fell, the girdle. A finger points at visitors to the Louvre; Madrid holds its chin; a lip pouts singly in Cambridge. But its nose is in the land of its carving, in a room built especially for it. The man who guarded it for years, seemingly reverent, one day tried to smash it with a sledgehammer. Other guards wrestled him to the ground, first turning his hands to rubble, then killing him. Now an elderly woman sits with her back turned to it—strict instructions—too weak to destroy it. She has a gun on her lap, ready to shoot madmen on sight. It is a voluptuous nose, speaking volumes on masonry, and culture, and a lack of words.

At that moment, reading the article, I ached for my father. He spoke to me only of strange facts, of ridiculous deaths, and suddenly I wanted him there, telling me that story; I wanted to tell it myself. I imagined he'd listen carefully, which shows you how little I was thinking of the actual man.

III

JACKIE FINISHED HIGH SCHOOL AND, WITH HIS EXCELLENT grades and extracurricular activities, won a full scholarship to the University of Maryland. Bobby gloated around Mike: his child was on his way to a happy, normal life.

I took a summer class called The Sociology of Deviance. The teacher and I were both amazed at just what the students found deviant, not to be borne in polite society: sneezing in libraries, littering, speeding, playing music for money in the park. The professor stood at the front of the room, almost pleading, saying, Please, don't any of you know drug addicts, alcoholics, religious nuts.

The heat in my attic was unbearable that August. One night, as I pulled my pillows downstairs to sleep on the couch, I heard a steady clattering from Dad's bedroom. I pushed the door open; a movie of a wedding played on the far wall. A man stood to the right of the projector's beam, his back toward me. I recognized Dad at once: he was drunk. He stepped into the jet of light, letting it hit him between the shoulders. I could almost see his muscles relax under it, warm as water. He took slow steps away from me. The movie covered him, found its way onto the wall. For a minute I thought it might be a film of my parents' wedding, then a custard pie streaked across Dad's back; no. Dad tried to examine the picture, blocking out whatever he put his face to with his shadow. I said, "Daddy."

He revolved slowly on a heel, wobbled, and looked into the eye of the projector, as if that's where the voice had come from. He smiled, maybe finally seeing what he wanted projected onto the whites of his own eyes.

Then he noticed me, and opened his mouth a bit. A derby hat floated on his shoulder. I waited for him to speak, to tell me the story of where he had been; or, at least, the life and death of the bemused, stony-faced, derbied man who now found himself on Dad's shirt.

What my father said was, "Please baby, later."

Later turned out to be breakfast. When I walked into the kitchen, Dad was in his old spot, Jackie on one side, Bobby on the other.

Bobby turned his face to mine. "Your father wants the house back."

"Not want," said Dad. "Need." Last night his face was mottled with baggy pants, indignant ladies, and fictional pies. Now I saw it. His nose had sagged, his eyes seemed further apart. The globe of his head had lost its pull, and things were drifting into space. "I need money," he said.

Jackie touched the edge of the table, then checked his fingers for splinters. "Well timed," he said. "Now that the children have been brought up."

"True enough," Dad said.

"They have been that," said Bobby.

"I didn't want to have to do this," said Dad. "This was not in my plans. I wanted you kids to have the house."

"Thanks for the loan," Jackie said.

"It's not what I want." My father tried to purse his mouth, but his lower lip had lost its elastic.

"I have a question," Jackie said. "Did you plan your departure? Did you invite these people here so that you could leave your kids with them?"

Dad laughed, then shook his head. Two very distinct gestures. "No. That's not it."

"What, then?" I asked, speaking for the first time that morning.

I recognized the look on his face: preparation for a truth.

He said, " 'Some have entertained angels, unaware.' "

"What's that," said Jackie.

"Bible," answered Dad.

"No joke. What does it mean."

"It's about hospitality. Being nice to the downtrodden," Dad said.

"It's about God," said Bobby.

That night, on my way to the attic, I heard Bobby crying, just as I had heard Candy every night for a month ten years ago. I still remembered those scattered, breathy sobs. Bobby's tears were soft and masculine. The long breaths he drew had all the wrinkles pressed out of them.

In the morning, like Candy, he was cheerful.

Bobby moved to Waltham; Jackie left for Maryland; Mike married his girl and jetted to Nepal. I got a postcard from him that said how happy he was to be in a foreign country for the first time in his life. It occurred to me that he'd been only twenty-one when he moved into our house.

I was tired of Boston, of knowing the bus schedule by heart, being able to direct tourists. Through my contacts at BU, I got a job at the University of Rhode Island and moved to Providence. I dreamt of things falling apart by pieces: the colossus, Dad's face, the house.

* * *

I last saw my father two years ago, halfway between now and then. I had driven to Boston to meet Jackie, who was on spring break; we went to see Bobby play in a Cambridge bar, one of Dad's old haunts. He had told Jackie that it was an old-fashioned Irish band, but it turned out to be, instead, Bobby, a guitarist, and an unhappy woman with a set of spoons who couldn't quite keep up with them. The place was packed, and Jackie and I squeezed into a table at the back. A waiter stopped to collect our cover charge and drink order. I asked for a vodka and soda, and knew I was in the right place when he said, "Large or small?"

Bobby was great. Better than that, he was handsome, his hair brushing the collar of his shirt. Halfway through a song, someone yelled, "Go for it, Bobby!" It was a huge drunken man who looked vaguely familiar—he might have stayed at the house for a few days, years ago. He toasted Bobby, smiling, in the middle of a serious crowd. Dad was sitting next to him, his hands holding a wrestling match with his chin, which wanted to hit the table and was winning. I decided not to tell Jackie, not because I thought seeing Dad would upset him, but because I was worried it wouldn't.

We had arrived late, and the band finished up the first set; Bobby leaned into the microphone and announced a short break. Jackie went up to chat. I stayed behind, not wanting to lose the table, not wanting to miss the waiter on the next campaign for drink orders. Jackie passed by my father, who saw him and just sat there. After a minute, he poked the man next to him and said something like, "Is that my boy?" The friend squinted at Jackie and Bobby, who were talking on the low stage, arms around each other. Then he shook his head.

I could tell Dad knew the truth, even though he hadn't seen Jackie for those two years, not since Jackie had gone to college, not since he had grown three inches and cut his hair very short, not since he called me up to say that as far as he was concerned, he was an orphan with many parents.

Finally, Jackie stepped off the stage and started to walk back to the table. Dad stood up just as Jackie passed him and presented himself the way long-lost relatives do in movies—teary-eyed, ready for embrace. Jackie shrugged, then hugged him, not bending down at all, not giving up the lean height that he made seem like politeness around his elders and charm around girls. For a second I said to myself, Look at that, look how Dad's shrunk—he's almost a foot shorter than Jackie now. Then I remembered he had never been tall.

They were about to part, their profiles turned to me. Dad's glasses were thick, rimless things. I couldn't see his eyes from this angle. All I could make out was that flash of incredulous blue that said, I do not understand what has happened here.

HERE'S YOUR HAT WHAT'S YOUR HURRY

AUNT HELEN BECK WAS square-shouldered and prone to headaches. She stretched out on sofas too short for her, and let her feet climb walls or rest on end tables or knock over plants. The children in the houses she visited told Aunt Helen Beck Stories, first to their friends, then to their own children, who sometimes got to meet the old lady in real life and collect their own tales, the same ones: the healing power of molasses; the letters she dictated to dead relatives. Her fondness for reciting James Whitcomb Reilly or any morbid poet with three names:

Edgar Allan Poe, Edward Arlington Robinson. She said she knew James Whitcomb Reilly when she was a girl in Indianapolis and had once presented him with a bouquet of flowers at a school pageant. He was drunk.

After a while, everyone Aunt Helen Beck knew was dead, and so she wrote a lot of letters, dictated to the children, who, despite being terrified of the enormous old lady on the sofa, loved scribbling down: "Dear Arthur. You have been dead fifty years and I still don't forgive you." Aunt Helen Beck would hold a small change purse in her hand and shake it as she spoke; it was leather gone green with age. Aunt Helen Beck said there were two pennies in it, though she would never show them to anybody.

"I have had these pennies for sixty-five years," she'd say. "I intend to be buried with them."

Aunt Helen Beck had many intentions about her death. She was about being dead the way some people are about being British—she wasn't, and it seemed she never would be, but it was clearly something she aspired to, since all the people she respected were.

I am your Aunt Helen Beck.

That was how she began every call, no matter who answered the phone. It was important to say it as if they should remember her, though of course, having never met her, they rarely did.

Aunt Helen Beck, they'd say. How are you?

Tell the truth, she'd answer, not so good. I'm in Springfield (or Delta Bay, or Cedar Rapids, or Yrma), and I need a place to stay.

Sometimes she'd explain that she was about to visit a friend who had now suddenly fallen ill. If she had stayed with one of their siblings, she'd mention that. They'd come in a pick-up truck or a sedan or a ramshackle station wagon, and when they spotted the one old woman likewise looking for a stranger, she could see their alarm. It was as if they were scanning a dictionary page for a word they'd just heard for the first time: Good Lord. You mean *that's* how it's spelled?

Aunt Helen Beck always liked that moment. She was bigger than anyone ever assumed she'd be; she looked as if she might still be growing, her hands and knees outsize, like a teenager's. People thought women were like dogs: the big ones were expected to die, until all that was left were the small, fussy sorts, the ones with nervous stomachs and improbable hair.

Then she got in the car with them and they drove home.

This time, it was a boat she stepped off, the ferry to Orcas Island, in Puget Sound. Already she could spot Ford and his wife, Chris: they kept still, looking through the crowd only with their eyes. Ford held his wife's hand. Aunt Helen Beck had stayed with Abbie, Ford's sister, a few years before. That's when she'd gotten Ford's address, and back then an island had sounded too far away to visit. Now she was beginning to run out of places.

Aunt Helen Beck walked straight up to them, one arm extended, without any doubt. In the other hand she carried a suitcase as if it weighed nothing at all.

"Ford," said Aunt Helen Beck. They both jumped. "And Chris." She bent down a bit to allow Chris a kiss on the cheek, but made it clear she did not want another kiss anytime in the near future. Ford took her suitcase instead.

She saw them take her in, her navy blue suit, clean shirt, none of the usual old lady fripperies: no perfume, makeup, or glasses.

Her gray hair was short and close to her head. She looked like a nun who had decided, after much thought, that as a matter of fact she'd always preferred cleanliness over godliness.

"You have a beard," Aunt Helen Beck said to Ford.

"Glory be," he said, touching his chin. "Actually, yes. I do."

"Your cousin Edward was fond of his beard, too. I always thought that bearded men were hiding something, but I have been assured that that's not true."

"I hope not," said Chris. She was a copper-headed, freckled woman dressed just like her husband, in blue jeans and a dark long-sleeved T-shirt.

"Just parked over here," Ford said.

Chris climbed in the bed of the truck. Ford tried to help Aunt Helen Beck up into the cab, but she wouldn't allow it. He walked around and got in.

"So." Ford tapped the steering wheel, then turned the key in the ignition. "How long do you think you'll be with us?"

Aunt Helen Beck looked at him. "Here's your hat what's your hurry, is that how it is?"

"No," he said. "No. I was just wondering—"

"Well, I don't know whether or not I like you. It would be premature for me to make a prediction. I might want to turn around soon as we get to your house."

"I hope," said Ford, a little sincerity forced into his voice, "that you'll give us more of a chance than that."

"Done," said Aunt Helen Beck.

She looked at his profile, at the sun coming through his beard. In fact, he was hiding things. There were acne scars on the parts of his cheeks that were out in the open; and it was clear that if you poked your finger straight into his beard, it would be a while before you hit any semblance of a chin.

"Here." Aunt Helen Beck reached into her pocket and pulled out a small framed photograph of a mustached man standing in front of a painted arbor. "For you," she said. "Your great-grandfather. My uncle Patrick Corrigan. Not my blood uncle, of course, but I was very fond of him always." She held it up. "You do look like him."

Ford looked at it out of the corner of his eye. "Nice-looking man," he said. "Thank you. Sure you want to give that up?"

"I always bring a present to my hosts," said Aunt Helen Beck.

They pulled up a rocky drive that jostled Aunt Helen Beck's bones, still sore from traveling. An old trailer flashed by, the round sort that had always looked to her like a thermos bottle, as if the people inside needed protection against rot. Then a house showed itself around a bend, halfway up the big hill. It looked like a good house, solid and small. Aunt Helen Beck had stayed in better, perhaps, but she had certainly stayed in much worse.

"This must be the place," said Ford, pulling on the brake.

She heard a child say to Chris, "You're ridin' in back like a *dog.*"

Chris barked a response, then came around to the door to help Aunt Helen Beck out. The child, who had white-blond hair halfway down its back, ran around with her.

"Who's that?" the child asked, pointing.

"Who are you?" Aunt Helen Beck replied, and then, because she couldn't tell, "Are you a little boy or a little girl?" They dressed them alike, these days.

"I'm a *boy,*" he said.

"Your hair's too long," she told him.

"I like my hair. My mother cuts it for me."

"Your mother is falling down on the job," said Aunt Helen

Beck. "Come to me and I'll do better." She grabbed her suitcase, which Ford took from her. "I'm your Aunt Helen Beck," she told the boy.

"He's not ours," said Ford, swinging the suitcase over his shoulder. "He lives in that trailer we just passed."

"Good," she said.

They went around back and walked into a bright kitchen, full of the sorts of long skinny plants Aunt Helen Beck had always distrusted: they looked like they wanted to ruffle your hair or sample your cooking. The boy followed them into the house. He flopped down on the couch; Aunt Helen Beck couldn't blame him. A child who lived in a trailer surely thought that furniture was a luxury.

"So," she said. "What's your name?"

"Mercury," he said.

"I beg your pardon?"

Ford shrugged. "His mother likes planets."

"I like vegetables," said Aunt Helen Beck, "but I wouldn't name my child Rutabaga. But—" she squinted at Ford, "—I suppose that someone named after a car isn't shocked."

"The theater, actually," said Ford.

"Huh," said Aunt Helen Beck. She turned to her niece. "Christopher Columbus, I presume?"

Chris just blushed.

"In my day," said Aunt Helen Beck, "we settled on a dead uncle and were done with it."

Mercury took off one of his shoes. "When you have children," he recited, "you can name them anything you want."

* * *

The house was a small prefab; Aunt Helen Beck had never heard of such a thing. The guest room down the hall was decorated with a number of faded bedspreads: on the narrow cot, as drapes, suspended from the ceiling like something in a harem. The furniture was otherwise sparse and functional; Ford explained that he had made some of it himself and was thinking of taking up caning. There was a picture window in the living room with a view of both Puget Sound and the silver trailer. According to Ford, Mercury's mother, Gaia, had casual attitudes toward marriage and having children. So far she'd had Mercury, Jupiter, Venus, and Saturn, and seemed bent on assembling her own galaxy, though God help the child named Pluto or Uranus. The kids were all as blond and airy as Gaia, and constantly orbited Chris and Ford's flower patch, dirty and nosy as trowels.

"Ford's cooking dinner tonight," Chris said. "What do you like to eat?"

"Nothing, really," said Aunt Helen Beck. "But I'll eat anything anyhow."

In the kitchen, Ford was pulling pots and boxes out of cupboards. "I'd thought I'd make some quinoa," he said. "The grain of the ancient Aztecs."

"Of who?" Aunt Helen Beck asked. She and Chris sat down at the kitchen table.

"Aztecs," said Ford. "Or. Incas? Ancient somebodies. The guy at the store told me. I think you'll like it."

"Because I'm ancient, no doubt."

"No, no," said Ford. But Chris laughed and touched Aunt Helen Beck's forearm lightly.

"No, really," Ford said. "Somebody ancient really did eat this stuff."

"But did they like it?" asked Chris, giggling.

"Not you, too," said Ford. "Okay. Rice? It's tricky, Aunt Helen Beck: we're vegetarians."

"As am I," said Aunt Helen Beck. "I knew you seemed sensible."

"Beans and rice it is," said Ford. He set out his things carefully: first garlic, then spices; he poured the rice into a glass measuring cup and then into a strainer. "No time to soak beans," he said under his breath, "so we'll just used canned," and Aunt Helen Beck could tell that he was a convert to careful diet: once upon a time he went through this sort of ritual with substances that were not so good for him. She had seen that sort of thing in plenty of houses.

"So where were you taking the bus from?" Chris asked her.

"From Vallejo." Aunt Helen Beck got up and opened a drawer, looking for silverware. When she found it, she started setting the table.

"Leave that," Ford said. "We'll do it."

Aunt Helen Beck ignored him. She said to Chris, "Usually I travel by car, but my car broke down about a month ago and I had to leave it behind."

"That's terrible," said Chris. "Are you going to get another one?"

"I can't tell. This car was a gift, so I suppose if someone wants to give me another I'll take it."

Chris tried to take a fork from Aunt Helen Beck's hand, but failed. "You're making me feel guilty," she said.

"Your guilt I can do nothing about," said Aunt Helen Beck. "The table I can."

"You're from Vallejo?" asked Ford.

"Heavens, no," said Aunt Helen Beck. "My niece Marlene lives there. I was just visiting her. And before that I was with Abbie, and before that I was with my dear cousin Audrey, who passed away."

"Oh dear," said Chris. "While you were visiting?"

"Yes, I'm sorry to say." Aunt Helen Beck straightened one of the placemats that was already on the table. "She gave me the car—she left it to me; she left everything to me. I think perhaps Audrey was my closest friend, though I didn't meet her until we were both grown women. In fact, I read her husband's obituary and realized this was a cousin and called her to offer my condolences, that's how we met. I visited Audrey often."

"How long had you been there when she died?" Chris asked.

"Five years. When you're seventy-four, the people you know are dying or dead. One gets used to it."

Ford rummaged in a kitchen drawer for a spoon. "Where do you call home now?"

Aunt Helen Beck picked up a fork and set it back down decisively. "All set here," she said. "Ready when you are."

After Aunt Helen Beck had cleared the table, washed the dishes, and wiped down the table, the three of them sat around the kitchen table. Aunt Helen Beck rattled her little purse.

"There must be a story behind that," Chris said.

"My brother made it for me." Aunt Helen Beck stopped shaking it but didn't open her palm to let them see.

"Another relative!" said Ford. "Where's he now?"

"He died very young. My brother," said Aunt Helen Beck, "was a child preacher. He toured the South with my father.

Beautiful child, Georgie. Famous, too. Before he died, he made me this purse for my birthday and put two pennies in it. I've kept it with me ever since."

"Nice to know there's spirituality in the family," said Ford.

Aunt Helen Beck waved her hand. "My father made him preach, and Georgie was smart and pretty. Children are not spiritual, in my opinion."

But the voice she used when she wanted to shut people up had no effect on him. "Why, Aunt Helen Beck," he said. "Children are spiritual creatures. It's why they're unpredictable."

"No," she said. "There's a difference between being spiritual and just being willful. Some people never learn that." She looked at him deliberately.

Chris laughed. "Don't get him started, Aunt Helen Beck. He's full of theories."

"So's Aunt Helen Beck, I have a feeling," said Ford.

She smiled back. "I'm sure we have a lot to talk about." She could tell he was flattered by that: he was the type of man who wanted to be invited to join every club there was. Even hers.

Aunt Helen Beck worked hard at all the things that convinced people to let her stay. She got up early to bake bread, examined the books that were on the shelves and referred to them in conversation. She did dishes immediately; cooked for herself; went to bed early and pretended to sleep soundly.

She charmed Mercury, at least. He adored her, and started playing in the yard less and in the house more. She instructed Mercury to behave, she threatened him with poems about goblins that stole nasty children, and he seemed eager to be taken, and asked her if she were the head goblin.

"He's a good kid," Chris told her. "Just restless."

"Perhaps," said Aunt Helen Beck, but she smiled. She was fond of Mercury, though the brother and sister old enough to walk struck her as colorless and dull. Children did not interest her until they were six: Aunt Helen Beck liked conversation.

She got that in abundance from Ford. He was a glib young man, too free and easy. Aunt Helen Beck had expected him to be reserved, since when she'd stayed with his sister he left a message on the answering machine: "Oh hell, Ab," he said. "You got a machine? Well. Hate these things. Guess I'll just write." Aunt Helen Beck had assumed that meant he wouldn't brook any nonsense, when really he just preferred his own special stock. He admired Indians—both sorts—and wrote poetry that he tacked to the doorjambs of the house, frequently addressed to "The Earth," or, "The Goddess." It took Aunt Helen Beck some time to discover that this second wasn't a pet name for his wife.

She was the reason Aunt Helen Beck wanted to stay. Chris stayed home all day to make her necklaces, which she sold through some of the shops and galleries in town. Sometimes, Ford helped with the beading, but Aunt Helen Beck noticed his impatience: he threw all the good beads together, and ended up with chunky clashed messes. His wife knew how to spell the dazzle with tiny beads and knots. Aunt Helen Beck noted with approval that Chris was quiet and perennially embarrassed: an attractive quality in a woman, and something, she knew, that had always been lacking in herself.

After a week, she let Chris catch her making a phone call in the kitchen.

"I thought I might come to visit," said Aunt Helen Beck into the phone. "Oh. Well, no, of course you're busy. Might I help? No, you're welcome, I just thought I might be useful. Some other time, perhaps. In a month or so." She hung up the phone.

"Aunt Helen Beck," said Chris. "You don't have anywhere to stay, do you?"

"I'm sure I'll find some place—"

"Stay here. We like having you, there's plenty of room—"

"Can't stay forever," said Aunt Helen Beck.

"Well," said Chris. She thought it over. "For a while, at least. For as long as you like. Why not?"

"Dear me," said Aunt Helen Beck. "You're sure to think of a reason eventually."

After dinner each night, Chris and Ford went in the living room and watched the sun set over the Sound and tried to get her to join them. They sat with arms around each other, and though Aunt Helen Beck did not strictly approve of that sort of public display, she did not object. She liked people in love: they were slow-witted and cheerful. They never asked her again how long she planned to stay.

Sometimes, she stood in the door of the living room, and the three of them looked at the trailer standing between them and the Sound. Ford liked to pretend he knew what was going on in there, and made up stories.

"About now," he said, "Gaia has fed them and bathed them—"

"Bathed them?" asked Aunt Helen Beck. "There's a tub in that tiny thing?"

"A little shower," he said. "Or she's taken them to the lake to swim. And one of them—probably Venus, since she's stubborn and a flirt—is refusing to get dressed and is bouncing off the walls, stark naked."

"And so Gaia is singing a getting-dressed song," said Chris.

"And Jupiter's crying," said Ford. "Because it's not a very good song."

Aunt Helen Beck shook her head. "All those people in one little house. I'm not sure I approve."

"What's to approve?" asked Ford. "She leads her life and she's happy. And they're good kids, so she must be doing something right."

"How does she make her way in the world?"

"Oh, the way anybody does around here. Part-time work, barter. She works a couple of days a week at the Healing Arts Center."

"Healing?" asked Aunt Helen Beck. "Physical healing?"

"Reiki. Rolfing. That sort of thing. Laying on of hands, really. Perhaps not so different from what your brother did, Aunt Helen Beck."

"My brother," she said, "was a child of God."

"Well, everybody's got their own idea of God," said Ford. "Anyhow, Gaia's good at what she does. She fixes things. Maybe—" he looked at her with teasing eyes, "—you should go to her sometime."

Aunt Helen Beck said, "I was not under the impression I needed fixing."

"Eat this."

Mercury closed his mouth around the spoon of molasses.

"Mmmmm." He licked the spoon all over, including the handle.

"You think that's good?" she asked.

"Yes," he said. Chris and Ford were in town, shopping, and Mercury had elected to follow Aunt Helen Beck through the house as she cleaned and straightened. His brother and sister had been outside, throwing dirt at the window, until she had dispatched him to tell them to stop.

"If you think that tastes good," she said, "I'm afraid something's wrong with you. You must be part dog, to think everything's good to eat."

"Maybe I am a dog," he said; he lay down on the living room floor, his hair fanning out behind him.

"How old are you, Mercury?"

"Seven."

"Do you know how to write?"

"Yes," he said peevishly.

"Well then." She looked around for a piece of paper. "Would you like to write a letter for me?"

"Who to?"

"Kneel down here," she said, pointing to the coffee table, "and I'll tell you what to say." She found a pencil and some lined paper in a drawer and gave them to him, then tried to stretch out on the sofa, a tiny loveseat. She bent her knees over the arm and let her feet dangle. "All right. Put down just what I tell you. Here we go. 'Dear Mac. Of course, we haven't spoken for a while. That is understandable.' Do you have that?"

"Yes." His head was bent over the paper and he was holding the pencil like a needle, very delicately. His hair, that ridiculous hair, hid his face. She imagined he was concentrating.

" 'But I need to tell you this: I'm still mad about what you said to me when last we met. Furious. You know what I'm talking about.' "

"What's in your hand?" Mercury asked, still writing. She figured he was stalling for time while he caught up to her words.

"It's a purse. A little boy made it for me a long time ago."

Mercury turned to look. "Any money in it?"

All little boys know what purses are for, thought Aunt Helen Beck: in each and every one a Fort Knox.

"Two pennies," she said. "Let's get back to work."

"Where does this guy live?" Mercury started writing again.

"He's dead," said Aunt Helen Beck.

"You can't write to dead people." He put down his pencil and turned around again.

"Why not?"

"They're *dead*."

"That only means they can't read," she told him. "It has nothing to do with what I can or cannot do. Let's see how you're doing." She sat up; the arm of the loveseat was cutting off the circulation to her feet.

He leaned away so she could see, and what she saw was this, in pale letters because he did not bear down: MERCURY MERCURY MERCURY KABOOM I LOVE YOU.

"Well," she said, because he had tried his best. "I might have put that last part down anyway."

In the morning, when she slipped her hand into the pocket for Georgie's purse, it was gone. She took her hand out of her pocket, put it back in, took it out, back in again. It was not in her pocket.

Not in her pocket, where it always was; not on top of the

dresser or tucked in her suitcase. Not anywhere in the kitchen, not even on the floor near the edges along the baseboards, which is where she was looking when Chris walked in.

"Aunt Helen Beck," Chris said, alarmed. "What's the matter?"

"Somebody's taken Georgie's purse. I can't find it anywhere."

"I'm sure it's around." Chris dropped to her knees beside Aunt Helen Beck.

"I can't find it." She hadn't ever been without the purse; it was one of her organs, it was vital. "I have to find it," she said.

"We will, we will." Chris had caught her worry. "I'll look in the living room." She crawled toward the other room just as Mercury came in the door. He laughed to see the grown-ups on all fours. Chris, looking over one shoulder, asked, "Have you seen Aunt Helen Beck's purse?"

"No," he said, too quickly.

"You're sure," said Aunt Helen Beck. She did not want to frighten him, but suddenly understood that he was the one who must have taken it. Who is as sneaky as a little boy? Who is more interested in other people's belongings?

"It's in your pocket," he said.

"No it isn't," she said, still on her hands and knees, still looking at him squarely. "If you have it, Mercury, I would very much like it back." She wished that just once, in all those houses she'd been in, she had picked up the child psychology book that was always sandwiched between Shakespeare and Tolstoy. Just use common sense, she'd always advised, but common sense, she now realized, had little to do with real life.

"It's not in my pockets," she said again.

"I don't have it," said Mercury, inching toward the door.

"Merc—" Chris began.

"I don't!" he yelled, and he ran out.

They sat back on their heels. Aunt Helen Beck rubbed the tops of her thighs slowly, in an effort not to cry. It didn't work, which surprised her.

"Oh, Aunt Helen Beck." Chris shuffle-crawled over to her, and laid one hand on her shoulder.

"What will become of me without it?"

"If he has it, I'm sure he'll bring it back. He's an honest kid, and he sees how much it means to you."

But Aunt Helen Beck could not see that happening. Little boys lose things. They trade them or bury them or give them to their sisters to chew on. The walls of the purse were the only walls she'd ever owned, and she'd allowed them to be taken away. She would have told another person in the same situation, You're allowed to be careless once in eight decades. She could not believe so herself.

"Aunt Helen Beck, your talisman," Ford said when he found out. "I'm so sorry. Maybe Merc's got it and he'll bring it back." He sat down on the loveseat beside her. "Listen. Maybe we can make a stand-in."

Aunt Helen Beck leaned away from him and looked out the window at the silver trailer, and envied the woman's life there. Gaia was surely surrounded by things she owned: big jars of rice, children. To keep your family in such a small place now struck her as intelligent; it was like making your whole life a locket.

"I don't mean replace," said Ford. "But it was a symbol. Now you need another symbol, something to stand for Georgie and how much you love him."

"Georgie Beck died when he was seven. There is nothing in this world that he touched except that purse."

"Earth's the same," he said. "Same then as now. We'll make a little pillow of earth."

Aunt Helen Beck turned to look at him, and was startled at how close he sat. She could easily have hit him. Some common damp dirt for Georgie? But then she saw Ford was sad and desperate over the whole thing and somehow wanted to help.

"No thank you," she said.

Thereafter, Mercury kept his distance. One little boy was dead and gone; the other had done something she was not sure she could ever forgive. Her anger at him did not make the loss of his company any easier to bear: you always miss the person who breaks your heart. A few nights later, she caught a glimpse of him outside of the trailer, staring up at the house, as if he were a miniature general considering the best means of attack.

Ford went down to the trailer to talk to Gaia, who said that she hadn't seen it, would keep her eye out. "She'll do her best," Ford said.

Even as he said it, Aunt Helen Beck felt herself change. She had been, up until that moment, in the same mood her entire life. The panic that engulfed her now was unfamiliar and frightening. She felt there must be a pill, something she could eat, that would clear it up. Or a pair of hands that put upon her would restore her to the way she used to be. But a pill worked its way through you, hands departed your skin. They were no replacement for the one thing she'd always owned.

Now she sat still to watch the sun set every night with Chris and Ford, and admired the family pictures that had always lined the walls. Those nights, she talked a streak, about nothing in particular. There was an affectionate recklessness to what she said: she spoke of people from her past, and family.

"I once knew a woman with twenty-one children," she said to Chris.

"Good Lord," said Chris. "That doesn't seem possible."

"It's true," said Aunt Helen Beck. "She was a collector. They weren't all hers; she just fancied them and took them in and when she tired of one, threw him out and got another."

"She sounds like a sad case," said Chris.

"Perhaps. Despite it all, I loved my mother."

"Your mother?"

"Yes," said Aunt Helen Beck. "We are discussing my mother."

And later, when Ford asked her what she did for Christmas as a child, she said, "Nothing. I always wanted to celebrate it, but my people are Jewish."

"What?" asked Ford. "What part of the family?"

"All sides. My grandfather was a rabbi." He looked confused, so she added, "Orthodox."

"I never knew we had any Judaism in the family," he said.

"You might not," she began, and then she caught herself. "You might not have been told," she said. "People used to like to cover that up, you know."

"But I thought your brother was a preacher—"

"Half-brother," she said quickly, her lightness gone. "And I don't want to talk about it. Have a care, Ford." Frequently she'd turn like that, from nostalgia straight into anger. Ford and Chris grew wary of her, and started going to bed earlier and earlier. She could hear them talk about her—her name again and again, because Aunt Helen Beck could not be reduced to a handful of pronouns. She didn't care to listen closely.

"We're glad to have you here," Chris would tell Aunt Helen Beck in the morning, coming in for a careful half hug. Aunt Helen Beck could feel heat coming off the younger woman's body. With her copper curls, her freckles exactly the same color, white skin underneath, Chris reminded Aunt Helen Beck of some pale cake left too long in the oven. She even smelled that way, delicate and warm, as if a sudden loud noise could make her collapse.

Did people always radiate such heat, or any heat? Did their temperatures vary? Aunt Helen Beck had never noticed before. She wanted to steal up behind Chris, or Ford, let a long breath loose across their skin to cool them before touching, cautiously, a quick furtive tap with her fingertips before allowing her whole palm to rest.

Sometimes, she would feel suddenly fearless and loving, put a hand on Ford's shoulder, give Chris a pat on the cheek, leave them notes in the bathroom signed with a heart. The one day they all went into town, she drifted off from them and returned with licorice, ginseng tea, a little trial-size packet of vitamins.

"Happy un-birthday," she said. "Have an un-birthday present."

Ford laughed, and said, "Aunt Helen Beck, you're all right."

"Just all right?" she asked. All he did was laugh again in his horsey way, but she really did want to know. She had tried all her life to be a good person, but how could she judge her success unless other people let her know? She knew she was not a good listener, supposed she got impatient at times. That's what having standards will get you, she thought: restless. It was one of the reasons she went visiting. Every person saw her a different way, and once she divined their opinion—bossy old lady or lovable crank or sometimes, she hoped, even nice plain honest woman—she wondered what someone else might think. She wondered if two people who knew her at separate times would agree.

Still, she felt now, for the first time, all it would take would be one person saying, Aunt Helen Beck, here's where you belong, and she'd stay in a minute.

She didn't hear the boy walk into the room until he said, "I want you to cut my hair."

"Hello, Mercury," she said. He hadn't been in the house in the two weeks since the purse had gone missing. She looked at him and hoped that he had it tucked in his pocket, though she still felt so wretched about its loss she was no longer sure even the thing itself would help.

"I want you to cut my hair, please."

"Why?" asked Aunt Helen Beck, but even as she asked, she eyed the blond fall of hair, thought about how it would feel, giving way to the pressure of a pair of scissors.

"Too long," he said.

"Get your mother to do it."

"She won't."

"Well then, perhaps you shouldn't."

"It's too long," he said. "Please? It makes me look like a girl. You said so."

"It makes you look like Mercury."

He took a deep breath. "Aunt Helen Beck, please cut my hair."

"What will you do with it?" she asked.

He pleated his nose at her.

"That's a lot of loose hair you'll have. Will you throw it in the ocean? Wear it as a bracelet?"

"I don't want it," he said.

"Well," said Aunt Helen Beck. "We'll see."

His hair was dry and light, like some rare delicate vegetable that couldn't possibly be nourishing but is rumored to cure cancer. She had to sit down to reach. He didn't make a noise, though she felt him wince every time he heard the scissors shut. She could only find the kitchen shears, and they were a little rusted at the heart.

"It's coming fine," she said.

She did not understand why she was doing such a thing, but it improved her; she felt herself return to normal every time the blades slid into a kiss.

"What will your mother say?" she asked.

"I don't care."

Finally, she finished.

"You're handsomer than I thought you were. Would you like a mirror?"

Mercury ran one hand up the back of his head, smiling at the bristle of it. Aunt Helen Beck knew a few things about hair cutting, and she realized it was not modesty when she thought: Well, I certainly botched this job.

"Feels weird," he said, which is when Chris and Ford came through the door.

"Shit," said Chris. She put her hands to her face, as if to steady her head.

"I like it," Mercury said.

"How do you know?" asked Aunt Helen Beck. "Run look in a mirror and then decide."

"Shit," said Ford.

"It's cool," Merc said, returning.

Aunt Helen Beck picked up Merc's hair, which she had braided and secured with rubber bands before she took the first cut. "I'm going to keep this," she said quietly. She started to look for a broom to sweep up the thin scraps on the floor.

Ford put his hand on Mercury's head; the boy leaned into the touch and rubbed his head against Ford's palm.

"I know you're upset," Chris said. She sat down at the kitchen table. "But why on earth?"

"He asked me," she answered. "You know I have never been able to refuse a child."

That evening, they approached her. "Aunt Helen Beck," Ford said. "I think we need to talk."

They took the loveseat; she sat in a chair across from them, feeling the curl of hair in her pocket.

"Tell me again," said Ford. "How are we related, precisely?"

"Your great-grandfather," she began, but then she realized it was gone. Usually, she knew everything, every uncle, but now she couldn't remember anything about Ford's family, and hers therefore, except that she imagined they were Irish. "He came from Ireland," she said. "He was a doctor."

"And?" said Ford.

"He was a magician," she said, changing her mind.

Ford sighed. "A witch doctor, maybe?"

"A flim-flam artist," she said. "A snake-oil salesman. Perhaps not really a doctor."

"No," said Ford. "Flim-flam runs in the family, huh?" He smiled; Chris poked him in the side.

"I called Abbie," said Ford, "and we discussed the possibility, and then I called the rest of my family and, Aunt Helen Beck— you're not related to us."

"Why, Ford."

Ford rubbed his beard. She could not tell whether he was enjoying this or whether he was truly sympathetic. "Maybe a family friend," he said. "I mean, maybe you grew up calling one of my relatives uncle. Family friend's enough, if you're a close one."

She knew that it wasn't. If it were, she could call up anybody and say, I once knew your mother. All that would get her was a cup of coffee, and besides, she'd have to know about college or DAR days or wasn't the wedding beautiful. She was silent.

"I thought so," Ford said.

"I can't believe this." Chris stared at the floor, then looked up. "You're a liar," she said.

Ford touched his wife's arm. "Now, listen—"

"You're one, too. You told me you remembered her. When she first called, you said, Oh yes, my dear Aunt Helen. And how long have you known this without telling me?"

"I'm not a liar," said Aunt Helen Beck.

Chris just shook her head.

"I took that picture you gave me out of its frame," said Ford, softly. "And it says on the back, Holland, school play. Even the guy's mustache is fake."

Aunt Helen Beck sat up straight in the chair, arranged her legs, smoothed her skirt.

"How did you choose us?" Ford asked.

"Well," she said. "I was at the public library, and Abbie had donated some magazines. They were good magazines."

Ford laughed out loud, but Chris looked bitterly disappointed. Which struck Aunt Helen Beck as unfair; she'd never claimed to have been related to Chris.

"I can't believe you made it all up," said Chris. "I can't believe you took advantage of us like this."

"I didn't make it all up," she said.

"You came in and told us sad stories that weren't even true. You made up this tragic dead brother—"

"Georgie Beck was real," said Aunt Helen Beck. "And everything I said I felt about him I did."

"Will you please, please tell us the truth, just for a minute?"

"It would be nice," said Ford.

Aunt Helen Beck looked at her and then at Ford and then out the window.

"It was my first visit. I'd heard he was sick—he was a famous child, and I heard this in my hometown, my real hometown. He'd preached there before and caused a sensation and people said what a shame it was. And so I went and knocked on the door and called myself cousin. I was a child myself, sixteen. Back then," she said, looking at them, "it was even easier. I really did nurse him, but he died anyway, and I took the purse—" Here she returned to the window, certain of herself in a way she had not been since the purse had been lost. "He'd made it for his brother, I think, and I took it and his name besides, and I left."

"You're a fraud," said Chris.

Aunt Helen Beck sat still. Flashes jumped off the water with such regularity that the sparkle looked somehow mechanical, as if it were worked by a crank. "He told me he loved me," she said. " 'God loves you, too,' but I told him to say the first part again.

"This is all the truth." She looked at them. "I suppose I'll leave in the morning."

"You don't—" said Ford.

Chris said, "It would be for the best."

They left her in her chair, said they imagined she'd rather pack alone. Though what she wanted to pack, of course, was nowhere in the house. She had never been caught before—never accused, anyway—and some part of her had stopped worrying about it. She couldn't bear the thought of leaving, of any more travel, certainly not without Georgie's purse. For a moment, she supposed the most useful thing for her to do was to die.

But she had no interest in dying. At least, she did not want to start soon. She felt her life was a course of study with the obvious terminal degree; to hurry it meant being somehow unprepared. She had asked them not to turn her in to the police, and Chris, who had softened a bit, said of course not.

"You're obviously harmless," she said before she went to bed. Then she said, "Be careful. You live pretty dangerously."

Aunt Helen Beck said, "I have been living dangerously for some time."

That night, she took a brass candlestick from the whatnot shelf in the living room; she always had to take something to give to her next host—a little gift, an heirloom. It made her feel like the families really were somehow related.

Leaving would not be easy. Usually, she left clean, as if each little life were a railroad car and she was simply walking through to the back. This time, she had left things behind: Georgie Beck, and information. She felt a wind across her legs; something new was starting. Aunt Helen Beck did not believe in fate, but she did think that you made mistakes according to what you wanted in your heart, and she could not understand what it was she wanted this time, what she was trying to tell herself.

She stayed up all night, wanting to see the light playing off the silver trailer one more time; she forgot that the sun rose on the other side of the island. Intent on catching the sun itself she barely noticed the growing light, as if she were a detective intent on nabbing a single criminal when in truth conspiracy was all around her. Suddenly it was morning. Time to go, she thought; she certainly didn't intend to face Chris and Ford again. Aunt Helen Beck picked up her suitcase, felt the candlestick roll in the bottom. Already she could tell she hadn't taken enough.

Outside the air was cold and wet. She began to walk down the hill, stepping sideways so she wouldn't slip in the mud.

"Hey," she heard somebody say.

It was Mercury. He stepped out from behind a tree, dressed in the clothes he'd been wearing the night before; a few hair clippings glistened on his shirt. Really, she thought, you could see why his mother kept his hair long: jug ears. Big as planets orbiting his head. Not a good-looking boy after all.

He scratched the back of his neck. "Hello."

"Good morning." Aunt Helen Beck set her suitcase down. "You're up early."

He blinked at her. She couldn't tell whether or not he was angry over the haircut.

"You're still asleep, looks like," she said. "You're grumpy."

He picked up a stone and turned it over in his hand. "Nope." Then he looked at her. "My mother says I can't come in till I grow some hair back."

"She left you out all night?"

Mercury shrugged and nodded at the same time, stepping closer. Aunt Helen Beck leaned down in the mud and put a hand on one side of the boy's head. He was damp to the touch, like something blown off a tree in bad weather. She saw in his eyes an old, familiar expression: I could go now, it wouldn't make any difference, my family album might as well be the phone book, so long.

She lightly took hold of one of those extraordinary ears—it was like a hand itself, like a purse, like something that could hold a great deal.

"Tell me, Mercury," said Aunt Helen Beck. "Tell me—are you fond of travel?"

THE BAR OF OUR RECENT UNHAPPINESS

THE DOG RAN INTO the bar.

"One of these days," George said, "I'm going to get that dog drunk."

"Don't you do it," I told him. "I know many men who'll protect that dog's honor."

"This dog?" said George. He leaned sideways off his stool to scratch her head. "Go ahead and tell him, Millicent. Everyone else knows what a slut you are."

George liked to blame things on the dog. If a bad song came on the juke, if the bar ran out of chips, if he couldn't find his coat, he yelled,

"Millicent!" Sometimes, the dog came running in and George would bawl her out. "Millicent, don't you know better?" The dog eyed him seriously, like somebody's mother.

Millicent sat out front of the bar sometimes like a human, leaning back on the step on her elbows, if dogs have elbows, if that's what they were. She seemed to be waiting for conversation, and on my way out I'd stop and tell her a very sad story. A dog knows tragedy, broken love affairs, missing children. She was a sand-colored bitch with a whorled, nubby stomach.

"Let me buy you a beer," said George. He was a young kid compared to me, maybe thirty, with one of those fancy beards that frames only your mouth, looks sloppy but takes daily careful shaving.

"I got to get going," I told him.

"Come on, Jake. One more."

I was becoming, for the first time in my life, a regular in a bar. Circumstances and George were to blame. Every Saturday, on my way to see my wife at the head-injury center up the street, I stopped for a drink. George was coming the other way; Mrs. Austin, Barb's roommate, was his mother.

Billy the barkeep set mugs down in front of us.

"So how's life treating you, Mr. J?" Billy asked me.

"About now, just fine. You?"

"Ah, not so good. This place in the summer, it's crazy. I'm thinking about going home."

"Don't do it," I said. "What can your fatherland offer you that Cape Cod can't?"

He thought for a minute. "More women and fewer fish."

"There's no fish in Ireland?"

"Not on every fuckin' matchbook, shopping bag, and menu."

"William," I said. "I want you to do me a favor. Tonight

after work, I want you to walk to the harbor and look out. Know what you'll see?"

"What."

"You'll see a moon as solid as a potato, with all the salt of the stars and all the salt of the sea heading for it. That should make you happy."

George laughed. "Don't listen to him, Billy," he told the bartender. "Go home if you want." He gave me a pat on the arm. "He's a nice man, but he doesn't understand anything about people."

This might have been true; the misunderstanding was mutual. Nobody knew what to make of me after Barb had her accident. I let my hair grow: I was fifty-five, white-haired, bald on top, and after a year, my hair brushed my shoulders. I dressed as neatly as I ever did—a necktie every day, I did my own ironing. I thought I looked fine. But when people saw me, they shook their heads.

There was a reason for the hair. Not slovenliness, but this: Barbara cut my hair on our first date. I had known her for a while before, and when I came nervously through the door, she was bold enough to say, "Look at that hair." She got out her scissors immediately. Once we were sweethearts, every time I saw Barb with scissors, I knew well enough to take off my shirt and sit down at the kitchen table. It had been years since I was in a barber's shop.

And besides, I hoped that she'd look at me one of these days, shaggy me, and she'd snap out of it, that I'd look so bad she'd have no choice. Stranger things have happened. I read in the paper that a man came out of a coma simply because his wife held his hand and barked like a dog.

It had been a year since Barbara stepped out into the street in front of our apartment building and got knocked into a lamp-post head first. The car got away, and most of Barb got away, too. When I came home—I was teaching—a neighbor had this to tell me: it was a blue Dodge four-door.

At sixty, Barbara was the oldest patient at Bayside, by a decade; her roommate, Mrs. Austin, was about fifty. Most of the patients were young victims of their own or someone else's recklessness: drivers who headed for phantom roads after too many drinks, motorcyclists who'd ignored the helmet law. You'd be surprised, though, at the recoveries. In the year I'd been visiting Barb, I saw dozens of kids carried in who within three months walked out. If you asked them, they might tell you they didn't feel all there, though you couldn't tell; some of them said that now they had to think hard before they spoke. Maybe that ended up to be to their advantage, there's no telling. If you were thick-skulled enough, you could bounce back completely in the first few months.

Barb was holding steady, and the doctors predicted she would for the rest of her life. It always hurt to see people discharged from the place, so even in the summer, when I didn't teach, I came on Saturdays. People were less likely to leave on week-ends.

Barb was now better than she had been at first; she talked some and one of her hands worked a little. The speech therapist agreed with the aides, insisted that most of what Barb said was just a collection of vowels with nothing behind it. I disagreed. She seemed to understand what was said to her, and sometimes answered with a certain look, a slow gesture.

Brain-damaged, badly so, though those were words I hated even to consider, especially since there was no knowing what they meant. The brain is a mysterious mechanism, said the doctors, and when damaged cannot be steadied with a splint or understood at all.

That afternoon, when I stepped off the elevator at the Bayside Head Injury Center, all I got was a giggle from the desk. Bayside was the only place anywhere in the state that had the facilities to take on a patient with Barb's sort of injury. Anywhere else would've just stuck her in a bed, no therapy, no extra attention.

"Hey, look," said a guy at the front desk. "It's the rock star."

I leaned on the counter. "You think so, eh? Think I look like a singing star?"

"You look a mess, is what you look," the head nurse said. "Honestly, Mr. Jackson, you're not a young man."

"Tell me something I don't know," I said.

I leaned on the nurses' counter to put off the walk to Barb's room; it was the hardest part of my weekly trip. The corridor was lined with young head-injury victims in their wheelchairs, a series of girls who looked weirdly alike. They were the bad ones; the ambulatory patients sat in the TV lounge or snuck smokes in the lobby. These were girls with faces off-center, one eye up at the ceiling and one at the floor, heads back, mouths startled open. Even the one black girl looked like the rest, as if their accidents made them sisters somehow. Every place you moved down that hall you caught somebody's eye.

"Barbara will be glad to see you," the nurse said in a voice that implied that she herself was not.

So I watched my feet on the way to Barb's room, feeling more than I wanted to the beer that George had talked me into. Barb was asleep. It was two in the afternoon, and Mrs. Austin, George's mother, had her face to me: she was in a coma, and they turned her every four hours, to avoid bedsores. She was a skinny middle-aged woman with a thin nose. I didn't know her story. George and I didn't talk about that. We didn't talk about what happened in the room or what had happened before. Mrs. Austin's radio was turned to the usual big-band station; an announcer was pitching a seafood restaurant.

I kissed Barb hello on the forehead. Her hair was long now, too, so beautiful it embarrassed me. When I first knew her, her hair was naturally red and artificially curly. I suppose I told her I loved it curly. The color went out of it eventually, and she never had it dyed. After a while, the curls took on a yellow, brittle tinge from all the processing.

Now it had grown free from the perms, steel gray, with just a hint of the old red. The small patch they'd had to shave had come in, too. The aides combed her hair away from her face and back to the pillow. Her hair looked rich and amazingly strong. There was a thin crease on her forehead, but it was from surgery and not the accident itself.

She didn't stir, so I just looked around the room I already had memorized. I saw Mrs. Austin's potted hyacinth, the photo of me and Barb stuck over Barb's bed. I ran my hand along the metal rail by Barb's arm, then covered her hand with my own. Frank Sinatra was singing from the radio: *Hey there, cutes, go get your dancing boots*. There's nothing like Sinatra to make a mortal man feel foolish.

So I watched the machine that clicked out Mrs. Austin's food, the gastronasal tube that fed her some sort of yellow liquid, a substance so creamy and familiar I felt by then I'd acquired a taste for it.

Then the aides came in. "It's time for Barbie to get up, stretch her bones," said one. She had a faint accent and was pushing a wheelchair; the other, younger, walked to the far side of the bed.

"I'll wake her," I told them. Barb was wearing a loose faded nightgown that I had brought in a few months before; it was hitched up near her hips. Amazing—I knew the muscles in those legs had given up, I knew they were not the legs that it was my pleasure once to know, and still they looked supple and sleek.

I took her shoulder and shook it gently. "Barbara. Time to get up."

Barb's eyes opened a little; she looked at me up and down, in slow motion, which was how she now did everything. Then she said something. Three distinct syllables.

I smiled. "What's that, Barb?"

My wife repeated it. This time, I leaned my good ear into her. Her voice was lower and rockier than it had ever been, and all the consonants were shaved off.

"She's not saying anything," said the aide.

"Yes she is," I said, embarrassed.

"What's it, then?"

Barbara sighed, and let out one syllable at a time.

"She's saying," I told them, "hello."

A lie, though I took heart in what she really said, because it meant she was paying attention. Still, I couldn't help feeling a little insulted.

What she was saying was: you're too fat.

Every week, I took the bus to the Cape; now, in July, I rode with the tourists headed to the resorts or for ferries to the islands. There was a motel across from the center that offered special rates to the families of patients. George had stayed there once or twice, even though he lived just forty minutes away. "Can't pass up a bargain," he'd say, laying money on the bar to buy us drinks.

Knowing George made things better. Six months before, our first meeting at Bayside had consisted of a few awkward moments in the room before he suggested a drink. Without ever discussing it, we somehow agreed never to visit the room at the same time again—hard to be friends at such moments, and besides, I don't think either one of us wanted to be one of those sad people who clings to other sad people. We never mentioned Bayside when we were together, just sat and chatted and knew the other one understood, that there was someone else in the world as unlucky as ourself.

I hadn't yet taken advantage of the family rate at the hotel. There was a slim chance that they might not consider me family. I call Barb my wife, but we were never actually formally married—I wanted to; she wasn't so sure. I met her through work. I taught history at a girls' private high school; she was a guidance counselor there for two years before she decided the girls were too poisonous to help. This was something I loved about her, though I can't tell you why it appealed to me: she did not much like other women.

"I hate people who complain," she told me.

"Who do you like?" I asked.

She told me she appreciated men, a no-nonsense crowd, in her opinion. She especially loved men who had bad teeth and sloppy table manners, who could not carry a tune but would try anyhow; men who didn't seem like they were paying attention but did. She loved men who did not cover a bald spot with trickery, who bought their own clothing and looked like it.

"Good heavens," I said. "Who are these people?"

"You," she told me.

The other people in our apartment building—mostly older folk—called us "the sweethearts," and not kindly. We had lived together for just ten years. This was a fact I generally kept hidden from my family, saying only that my wife had decided to hold on to her maiden name. Barb had a grown son, but I had power of attorney. Now the son, Roger, called from time to time and said I should just give word if I needed anything. By which he meant money.

I tried not to miss Barb too much, since she hadn't exactly left me, but let's face it, there was no easy way. I tried not to feel like she was an utterly different thing in that bed; I wanted to believe that she was just Barbara, with a few alterations. But if there was a way to make me think that, I hadn't figured it out.

How can I say this without sounding hard? I hated visiting her, I really did. I was relieved when I left. I made myself stand there and talk to her for at least an hour and a half every visit, or stand there at least. If I could think of some little topic of conversation—something a neighbor had done, an interesting weather report—I would prattle on. Mostly I stood and looked. Sometimes I'd start to be serious, I'd be ready to say, Darling, this is a bloody shame for both of us, don't think I don't know that. But since talking to Barb felt like talking to myself, I could never do it. I'd try to hold her hand. Sometimes she held on to me, sometimes she pulled her restless hand back, let it wander up and down the edge of her blanket.

The apartment, when I got home from Bayside, seemed as usual unfamiliar, shabby. I tried to keep it clean. I hadn't the knack for it. For a while, I had a woman come in once a week, but it got to me. There were all my habits in plain view, and since our accident I'd been piling up the bad habits. A gallon jug of burgundy, a bottle of cheap whiskey, garnet rings from wineglasses all around. A teacup sat on the table, a cigarette stubbed out in its center. I'm not much of a smoker, but I succumb sometimes.

I sat at the kitchen table, found a loose crumpled cigarette in my jacket pocket, and stuck it in my mouth without any idea of where a match was.

I am a man of many small mistakes. I am not competent. This is not harsh self-judgment, it is a fact. I have burned food all my life; I wear spotted clothing without noticing; I botch household jobs. I can't fill out a check right the first time. I am not an expert at day-to-day living. This can't be turned into anything good—you can't say I'm being cautious or that I'm thinking deep thoughts—there's no excuse for why I do things this way. I never learn. Behind every picture hanging on my wall is a pattern of dark circles where the hammer hit before I managed to sink the nail.

Every picture before Barbara moved in, that is. Before we met, I imagined that efficient people would want nothing to do with me. Other teachers would tsk-tsk as I tried to make copies in the school office, turning what I copied the wrong way, accidentally running off twenty muddy unreadable versions. People wanted to take things out of my hands and do them right.

This included Barbara, but there was love behind it. "Here," she said. "Let me." Suddenly, it made sense that I would need in my life someone who managed things, who knew about air conditioners and dry cleaners.

On a Sunday, a week before our accident, I lounged in bed. Barb was as usual up early, getting dressed. Her bra was small for her—she'd put on some weight—and it cut into her breasts a little. That she did not notice pleased me. She never consulted a scale, never wore unforgiving clothing that would tell her about a few extra pounds. I thought: I know her body better than she does, the grayish thick skin at her elbows, the topography of her hands. This is what I know best. This is why I'm needed.

"I'm off to the store," she said that morning, pulling on a T-shirt. I could see the same effect through the red cotton, an extra gentle swelling across the chest.

"Well, come here before you go," I said, and lovely literal Barbara threw back the covers of the bed and crawled in next to me, fully clothed. I could feel the fabric of her clothing all along me, the tips of her shoes against my legs. I put my hand on her stomach, and almost told her how I loved those extra pounds. But I didn't. It seemed at the time more my department than hers.

"Okay," I said, and put out my hand. It was a game we played: I'd say, Here, give me your elbow, or hip, or knee, and offered the palm of my hand. She'd scoot something closer, and bend.

"You're terrible," she said, offering her hand, palm up. It opened and closed inside of mine. "Is that all I am to you, a set of knuckles?"

My eyes closed, I said, "Darling, what's a body without hinges? Just a shut door."

Now her weight was gone, and the rough skin, too, rubbed away by the Bayside's loving lotions. I was still the expert, could tell anyone who asked what Barb was doing at that very minute: speech therapy, dinner in half an hour. And Barb would say, "Why is he telling you this? I can tell you're not interested." And now when we saw each other, I stood up and she lay in bed, perpendicular, two sorry planes that at best could meet at one sorry spot.

The next week was just a week, the regular progression of days between visits. I took out the trash, read newspapers, thought about making some phone calls but didn't. Sometimes I thought about ringing up George Austin—he lived in Plymouth, I could have found the number—but what would I say? We had only bar chat between us, and in a bar that was enough: he was the only thing that made those Saturdays different from one another, not just a bead on a string. But he was a casual acquaintance. I didn't know what he really thought of me. I'd spent my life piling up casual acquaintances, only to find, when I met Barbara, that all those friendships seemed flimsy and superfluous.

Still, I was glad to see him the next week at the bar; I always was. The minute he walked in he yelled, "Another drink for Jake," as if we hadn't stopped at three drinks the week before. Lately, he'd wanted me to drink more and more. I almost asked him, What's going on here? But I was sure he'd make a joke, buy me another beer. "I want you to be happy," he'd say, laying his money down. George did not respond to serious inquiries.

"So, Jake. What's new?" he asked me after we'd finished a drink.

"Not a damn thing," I said. "And you?"

He smiled. "Oh, you know," he said. He crossed his right arm over his chest and tapped his left shoulder, and thought. "Nothing I can't handle."

"Good," I said.

"Yeah." Still holding his shoulder, he shrugged. "I guess." Then he smiled at me. "You're a good man, Jake. You're a rare bird."

I felt a little uncomfortable. "You too," I said. "The good part, I mean." I glanced at my watch. "About time. See you next week."

"Already?" George asked. He looked at his watch, too, got off his barstool, got back on. "Okay. Be seeing you."

When I first walked into the room at Bayside, all I noticed was that Mrs. Austin was gone; I figured that maybe they'd taken her down to the common room, though I'd never known them to do that. Then I saw that her side of the room was completely clear: the machine, the hyacinth, the radio. She had disappeared.

Barb was awake, propped up with pillows. I kissed her absentmindedly, and she gave me back one of those slack-mouthed puckers she still handed out sometimes. "Your roommate move out on you, Barb?" I asked.

She seemed to shrug.

"Boy," I said. "I didn't even know she was sick." George had not said a word to me. Clearly, he was right: I did not understand people. I reviewed the afternoon, could see no clues.

I sat down on Mrs. Austin's stripped bed, feeling a little panicky, the tops of my feet full of prickles. Then I grabbed the button on the string that called the nurse and pressed it.

Then I pressed it again.

The head nurse came by in a hurry. She was one of the sourest people who worked there, a huffy young woman who had no time for anyone. "Thought it might be you," she said.

"What happened to Edith?"

She glanced at her watch, then closed the door behind her. "It's this way. Her family decided to move her."

"They weren't happy here?" I asked. "George never said a word. I see him all the time—"

"Well, he couldn't say anything, not till things were settled and done. They've talked it over with their pastor, and with us. They've decided to withhold feedings."

"I don't understand," I said.

She spoke a little louder. "They're taking out her feeding tube. Our board of directors wouldn't allow them to do it here, so they took her to a place in New Hampshire. Her son did want you to know."

"I know George," I said.

"They had to take her out in the middle of the night. They didn't want it to get into the papers, because you never know who's going to make a fuss. It happened to us once before," she said. "We're very careful now. We asked them not to tell anyone until the move was over."

"I saw him *today,*" I said.

"Huh. All I can tell you is what I know," she told me. "He told me he would tell you."

I nodded.

The nurse took my hand in a pretty courtly way for a sour young woman. "It's a crying shame." She patted my knuckles. "They'll be moving in another woman Monday."

I heard somebody coming down the hall, a man who gallantly said to each of the girls in their wheelchairs, "Hello. How are you. Afternoon." His sneakers squeaked at the door of Barb's room; his hand clicked against the metal doorframe.

"Aha," he said. "I'm not too late."

"Too late?" I said.

"I was afraid I'd miss you," said George.

I stared at him. He looked ten pounds lighter—too skinny to

stand, I thought—but handsome, handsomer than I'd known he was. Then I realized it was this room's fluorescent light, good strong light. I wasn't used to that. He was young.

He smiled, embarrassed.

"I'll leave you alone," the nurse said. She pushed out past George, into the hall. He took a few steps in.

"I hope you don't mind," I said, and I put my feet up and lay down on the bed of a woman I'd met many times and never. My heart rode in the dumbwaiter of my stomach. There I was, fifty-five years old, the entire world of emotions open to me, and what had I picked? I could have grieved, been sympathetic, could have frowned in disapproval, felt comfort for the family. I longed even to feel unsure. Instead, I felt a sickening jealousy creep up through my jaw and into my face.

"Swear to God," George said, "I wanted to tell you. But it's like I'm a different person at the bar, you know?"

I didn't say anything.

"Here's where I talk about my mother," he said. He pointed at the floor. "Correction: I talk about my mother everywhere. Except with you at the West End. I kept trying, but, you know—"

I looked back up at the white ceiling and tried to have a thought that would take away the jealousy. Sometimes when I caught myself reminiscing about Barb, a condition I knew would only lead me to more whiskey and tears, I imagined myself, my whole self, slammed in a door. I concentrated on what that would feel like. Usually it worked, but not now. Now I was gripped by a new feeling, something I had never felt before. I didn't know what would take it away.

"It's hard," said George.

This is the morbid thought I had instead: the driver of the

blue Dodge, the one that hit Barbara, might end up in Bayside. You read the newspapers after a murder, and they quote the victim's family, who want either to forgive or kill the murderer. I had simply refused to think about the driver, but suddenly the driver was the only thing I could think of. Say it was a woman—she might move into the bed I was lying in. She'd have to have been a reckless driver, and that was the main trade of Bayside. Or if the driver was a man, his girlfriend could take the bed. Maybe the Dodge would try to race through a railroad crossing and not quite make it; he'd be killed and she'd be here. Or he would escape with a few cuts and she'd be here. Neither way quite satisfied me. I played it both ways in my head, I mean I imagined everything: the back of the car clipped and spinning on the tracks, a thin body thrown through a window. In my head she sailed, already prone, already ready for bed.

"Are you okay, Jake?"

"I'm so sorry about your mother," I said, ashamed I hadn't said it earlier. After all, this happened to him, his family, not me.

"Well, we realized it was inevitable," he said. "You know how it is. You get resigned. God helps you through."

"Yes," I said, though I thought no such thing. I'd never before heard him talk such trash.

"I'm sorry we didn't get a chance to know each other better," George said. Indignant, I looked at him to reply, and saw that he was speaking to Barbara, who was asleep and could not hear him. But of course, he thought that was usual, the dreamy look that does not let you know anything, that lets you translate hope anyway you want. She hears you or she doesn't hear you, whatever makes you feel better.

He rubbed his eyes beneath his glasses.

"How long?" I asked him.

For a minute he didn't understand; then he did. "Well, we just moved her last night. It will take a while. We're still giving her water." He rubbed his face again. "My sisters are there now. She has company. Me, I'm beat." Then he looked at me. "You don't look so great yourself, Jake."

I sat up, and he sat down next to me on the bed, where the nurse had been.

"You want to go have a drink?" he said. "It's been, what, forty-five minutes? About time, huh?" There was an almost mischievous sparkle in his eye, and I saw the truth: he was happy. Something had happened. Something had changed for him, and it gave him power. His carefree life in the bar was spilling out.

He touched my shoulder, just the ends of my hair. He said, "You know, there's a great barbershop down the street, one of those guys who's been cutting the town's hair for years. I love that stuff. Could use a trim myself. Wanna go?"

Lying comes quick to the good-looking, to the relieved, have you noticed? George's hair was bristly, just cut. But I realized he was a young man who had recently gotten into the habit of taking care of people, and it seemed like a duty. Sweet, somehow, too.

"Just a drink," I said.

He stood up and walked to Barb's bed. He held her fingers, tight, then turned her hand over. "Goodbye, Barbara," he said. George kissed her knuckles, dropped her hand, and took three steps away, then came back and kissed her hand again. Like she was some kind of queen. It struck me as overly familiar.

"'Bye, honey," I said. "I'll see you next week."

"Well," whispered George. "It doesn't seem like she's suffering."

Her eyes opened, and it seemed to me that I'd been wrong, that she hadn't been asleep during all this, that she had been listening carefully and biding her time.

She let out a string of vowels, the same one with the same inflection twice.

"I know, baby," I told her.

"What's she saying?" George blushed. I'd never before thought of him as a man who could blush.

"I don't know." But the fact of the matter was I did. The speech therapist might not be able to understand her, but I could, and I imagined that when that quack said to her, "The rain in Spain," etc., it was this she repeated back, and he took it as nonsense.

She was saying, very politely, *I'd like to die, too.*

Billy the barkeep waved when we came in the door. Millicent was sitting in the middle of the room.

"Millicent," I said to the dog. She wagged her tail as she sat on it. "You're a nice pup." I scratched her ears. This didn't seem to satisfy her, and as I walked past, I felt her look at me over her shoulder.

I sat down at the bar, waiting for George to say something. I wanted a cigarette, but I remembered George hated the smell. I knew that much about him. Then I decided I didn't care, found a cigarette, and lit it. I took a sip of the wine Billy served me and felt the muscles beneath my tongue relax a little bit.

George sat down next to me. He tried to pay for the wine, but I wouldn't let him.

I smoked several more cigarettes and drank four glasses of wine straight through and felt drunk. I am not really a drinker, as Barbara, if she were there, would have been happy to announce.

I burned for her to be there to bawl me out, to tell me firmly, Enough. Don't wallow in your own eccentricities. I won't stand for you doing this, my friend, so you'd better reevaluate. I burned for all the things I could not let myself fully imagine, because if I started to, if I did for a minute, well. I wasn't allowed to grieve for her and I wasn't allowed to recognize her and my memories were in cold storage.

George was talking in a soothing voice. I wanted to hit him. Who are you, I wondered, to take on the troubles of the world when you have plenty?

"It's all very hard," he said.

"Oh, buddy," I said to him, "how would you know?"

He looked at me, shocked, and I saw that George was drunk, that he was crying, that he was talking about himself.

"Oh, Lord," I said. "Oh, George. I'm so sorry." And then I took his hand. He let me hold it. It was an old rough thing on a young man.

Outside, the sun was setting, through clouds so thick and faraway it looked like a weathered billboard.

"For a while I felt better," he said. "And now I feel worse."

"The real thing," I said, very carefully, and I was surprised at how blurred my speech sounded, "is that we never found the guy. I keep looking, you know."

"Okay, Jake." He was caught in his own grief. I could tell he didn't know what I was talking about.

"It's a matter of looking harder." It was suddenly clear to me. We find the guy driving the blue Dodge, and our problems are over. He could tell me things. And I could tell him—wouldn't he have to listen to me? Wasn't he the one person in my life who would be obligated? I'd lost anybody else, that was clear. But I would practice. I'd tell the whole story to George, that very night, would make him listen to it all. Then I would tell Billy, and then Millicent, and whoever I sat next to on the bus, and when I got home I would call up Barb's son, and by that time, by morning, I'd have it down, every detail.

"My mother slipped in the bathtub," George said. "In my bathtub, when she was visiting me. You wouldn't think such a little thing could lead to all this."

I could smell the smoke in my hair, and the wine on my breath, and was worried that if George could smell it, he wouldn't listen. So I swept my hair away and spoke tight-lipped. I was aware, suddenly, that we were both unabashedly teary-eyed, that Billy was saying, "Gents, you okay?" and I thought: too much to drink, we're sad men, we're tired.

"I'm going to find him," I assured George Austin, shaking his hand.

"Yes, Jake," he answered. His glasses were off and he wouldn't look at me. "You will."

MERCEDES KANE

WHEN SHE WAS A little girl in the 1940s, my mother read books about child prodigies and got jealous. She wanted to be one herself, but her memory worked in all the wrong ways. She remembered bus routes, birthdays, and the latest hairstyles; she forgot Latin, the Moonlight Sonata, and how a transistor works. You can't be a genius, she told me once, if you forget what it is you're geniusing, and if you're stupid, you might as well be absentminded.

"No point in holding on to foolishness," she said.

She knew it didn't work that way, mourned what she forgot and despised what she remembered. Sometimes I caught her in the kitchen, singing along to one of my father's tapes of old rock and roll. She'd dance a little, or chop onions in time. Once I caught her standing stock-still in the middle of the room, both hands over her heart, like some crazy teen idol.

"Who knows why I remember all the words to *that,*" she said, scowling at the Everly Brothers' voices like her memory was their fault. "A waste of brain space."

But words stayed with her like that; she had a good head for poetry, too. When I was small, she'd recite poems to me while I was in the bathtub, sometimes from books, sometimes from memory. Her favorites were by Mercedes Kane, one of her child prodigies from the forties, who wrote beautiful poetry at the age of eight—long fantasies about invented towns and country dirt roads, sonnets about famous painters. Mama first read about her in the *Register* when she was seven: they were the same age, and Mercedes Kane lived in Chicago, a few hours away. When Mama went to visit her Chicago cousins, she'd look around the streets, sure she'd recognize a girl genius. The *Register* said that Mercedes Kane could multiply five-digit numbers without even thinking, that she knew six real languages plus Esperanto, that she was a serious little girl, and quiet. We had a book of her poems; it was wrinkled with steam from my baths.

The Quiz Kids were on the radio around then, too, but my mother said they didn't interest her. "Show biz," she said to my father, who himself had been on a local kids show in Des Moines. He had won seventy-five silver dollars. One time, after they'd had a fight, my father snuck into my room and told me angrily: "She tried out for the Quiz Kids, and didn't get on. Sour grapes."

Still, Mama thought she had what it took, or could have had with the right attention. She blamed her parents, her mother in particular. "I was musical, I was mathematical," she said to Grandma Sarah one Thanksgiving. "I taught myself to read when I was four—you could've taught me even earlier."

Grandma just told her how bad it was to push children, and with eight kids, who had time, anyhow? Who knew which ones would be intelligent and which ones would be my Uncle Mark? Child prodigies were unhappy, she told Mama, they never got to play, they almost never did anything great when they were older. They got depressed; they committed suicide.

My mother didn't believe that. She was sure she would've been great in her twenties, thirties, forever, if she had just been encouraged to greatness early on. She wouldn't have gotten depressed—she was unfailingly, antagonistically pleasant. She was unlucky enough to be the only cheery member of her immediate family, and the only one without a sense of humor. She suffered around my father and me. If she was cheerful, we became angered by her cheerfulness and made gloomy jokes; if she tried to joke in return, we'd look at each other and roll our eyes. She was neat and organized; on vacations, my father and I wouldn't get out of our pajamas for days.

She divorced my father when I was eight. She couldn't divorce me. After the split, she taught French at a Catholic girls' school. She tried to teach me, too. It was impossible. She would've liked me better if I had been smart, but I wasn't.

"You were a lazy baby, Ruthie," she told me. How do you answer to that? She gave up on me, and dreamed of her own childhood, which had been happy. Her father was a quiet man who had loved everybody and died at forty-five, before we had a chance to meet. I never knew how to refer to him. Grandpa?

Your father? Grandma Sarah's husband? She told me once that he would have asked me to call him Sidney, but calling a relative, an old man, a dead man, by his first name seemed impossible.

I was eleven when Mama found Mercedes Kane at the grocery-store lunch counter and brought her home. It was an astounding thing to do.

Saturday morning, I sat on the sofa in our apartment watching "Abbott and Costello Theater" on Channel 13. I watched it every week, had all the routines memorized.

Mama walked in, leading a strange woman by the hand.

"Ruthie, this is my friend Mercedes. She's going to stay with us awhile."

The name sounded familiar, but this woman—a friend? That had to be a lie. My mother's friends were as neat as she was and had names like Rita, Harriet, and Frances. This woman was small and puffy; she had long gray hair that was combed straight back and looked tangled. Her dress was a plain faded print; her feet were done up in men's slippers over several pairs of socks. And she was smoking: none of my mother's friends smoked.

My mother put her hand on the woman's shoulder and leaned down. "Would you like to take a bath, Mercedes?"

Mercedes shrugged my mother away. "Do I have to?"

I laughed, because she sounded just like me.

"Wouldn't you like to?"

"You're the hostess."

Mama led Mercedes down the hall to the linen closet. I knew she was taking one of the towels out, plumping it proudly. My mother bought expensive new towels every few months; it was a luxury she approved of.

I heard the bathroom door close, and Mama came back.

"Do you know who that is? Mercedes Kane! We have her poetry. This is *her*. I found her at Dahl's."

"The smart little girl?"

"That's her. She was sitting at the counter, eating a hamburger and smoking, and she was reading one of her own books—*The Rose in the Garden,* that's the one we have. I was having a cup of coffee, and I saw it, so I started to talk to her. I didn't know it was her, and she didn't say anything. She said her name was Mercedes, but she wouldn't tell me her last name. I asked her, you know, if she was the little girl I read about in the paper. 'Who?' she said. I said: math genius, language genius, girl who went to the University of Chicago when she was eleven? She said no. 'I used to write a little poetry,' she said."

"Maybe it's just somebody pretending to be her."

"No, I know it's her. I'm sure of it. So I invited her to stay here awhile."

"Doesn't she live somewhere?"

"She says she's got a room, but she won't say where." Mama sat down on the edge of our old chaise longue. "I can't believe it. Right here, Ruthie, Mercedes Kane. Now, don't mention what you know about her. She doesn't want to talk about it. She's just my friend, okay?"

"This is weird."

"It's okay, it's fine."

I'd never seen my mother so excited. She fussed around the living room, scratching her forehead, rubbing her chin. I think she was trying to look smart. Every now and then she stopped in the middle of the room, put her hands on her hips, and smiled. After a few minutes, she flipped off the TV.

"Hey," I said, although I had stopped watching it a few minutes before.

"Honestly, Ruthie. You'd think you didn't know how to read or write or walk around. There you are, every day, with your mouth open. Your brain will waste away."

"I'm not here every day. I don't watch that much."

"Any is too much."

"Mama."

"Don't whine."

Mercedes came creeping in from the hall, wrapped in my mother's toweling robe. She was still smoking; it was like she didn't stop for a minute, not even for a bath. Even though her hair was wet, it didn't look clean. But her cheeks were bright pink—healthy pink—underneath all that tangle.

"You look much happier, Mercedes," my mother said. "Would you like a cup of coffee or tea?"

"A cup of black coffee, please." She bowed oddly from the waist. The bath had washed away her rudeness.

"Well, it was a fast bath, anyhow," said Mama. "Was it a good bath?"

"Yes, thank you. Nice big bathtub."

"That's true. Old-fashioned. They don't make them that deep anymore. Mercedes," my mother said. "You have just the prettiest coloring. A healthy glow, I'd call it."

"Yes, that's one thing." Mercedes squinted at the smoke at the end of her cigarette. "I can't ruin my health, no matter how hard I try."

That evening, when I walked into the kitchen, my mother was speaking French. Mercedes peered into her coffee cup, smiling and nodding. I could tell Mama was asking a question, but

Mercedes didn't respond, and finally my mother rolled out one set of words several times, adding "Mercedes" in her fancy accent. Finally, in exasperation, in her regular voice, she said, "*Mercedes.*"

"Hmmm?"

My mother repeated her French question.

"Are you talking to me?"

"I have been, for the past five minutes."

"Oh, I wasn't paying attention. I thought you were talking on the phone."

"But I've been right here in front of you, honey. I'm all excited to really talk French with somebody, it's been so long."

Mercedes shrugged one shoulder and tilted her head. "I don't know any French."

"Oh, I'm sure you do," Mama said. "I mean, I remember reading—"

"That was someone else, I'm sure. All I know is English, and I'm not too handy with that."

"But I remember," said Mama. "The papers all those years ago. You spoke eight languages. You even made a language up."

"No." Mercedes frowned. "Somebody else."

"It wasn't," Mama insisted. "It was you, Mercedes. I remember."

"There were a lot of little girls in the news."

"I wouldn't forget. I wanted to be like you."

"Maybe one of the Dionne quints."

That made Mama laugh. "I wanted to be a quintuplet, too, but I figure I can't blame my parents for that. But you, you were a mathematician—"

"No. I can't even add. I've barely got a brain."

"But you wrote those poems, right? You admit that."

Mercedes rested her tongue on her lip, as if she were wondering whether an admission would taste good. "No," she said finally. "I'd like to be able to say I did . . ."

Mama leaned against the table, sighed, and watched Mercedes with one eye half closed, the other one open as far as it would go. I recognized the look: It said, How-stupid-do-you-think-I-am-I-know-you-did-it. I got it when I broke something and blamed the air, and I got spanked. But Mama just shook her head now and said, "Let me take you out to dinner tonight. You and me and Ruthie. Anywhere you like. How about the Hotel Fort Des Moines? You can borrow one of my dresses if you want."

"How about Noah's for pizza?"

"Oh, for Pete's sake, Mercedes, I want to take you someplace nice, someplace we'll enjoy ourselves."

"I'll enjoy pizza," Mercedes said firmly.

"But—"

"I wouldn't like the Fort Des Moines. I hate the downtown."

"Pizza sounds good," I said from my spot near the door.

They turned and looked at me, surprised.

"There you go," said Mercedes.

"Pizza," said my mother. "Okay."

So we went to Noah's, where Mercedes drank cup of coffee after cup of coffee, Mama keeping pace with glasses of red wine. At the end of the meal, Mama stood up, held her purse to her belly with a fist, and asked Mercedes if she wouldn't mind driving.

"No problem," said Mercedes. She drove very carefully. In the garage at home, she got out and gave the hood of the car a pat.

"Never drove a standard before," she said. "Just a matter of coordination, isn't it?"

Mama went to bed right away. I sat in my room at my desk, drawing cartoons to amuse myself. I had an old Fred Astaire record on the player. It had been an inheritance from my father's parents, the only thing I had wanted from their house. I felt soothed every time I listened to it.

Mercedes came to the door and knocked on the frame. "Who's this singing?"

"Fred Astaire."

She looked serious for a minute. Then she said, "Oh," smiling. "You're too young to know who he is."

"I got it from my grandparents. It's my favorite."

"I'm old enough to know, and even I don't."

"I watch his movies on TV all the time. You seen them?"

"No. TV's a habit you have to get into. Never did." She scratched her elbow with the palm of her hand. "Ruthie, do you have a radio I can borrow? I like listening to the talk shows."

"All I have is a clock radio. Mom's got a portable."

"She's asleep. I don't want to bother her."

"Take the clock radio. Tomorrow's Sunday. I don't need it."

"Thanks." Mercedes took the radio off the nightstand and followed the cord to the wall. "Your mother's an interesting lady. Very bright."

"Guess so," I said, turning back to my cartoons.

"She knows what to think. Things don't just pop into her head, you know?" She paused. "What're you working on? Homework?"

"Nope. Nothing."

"Oh." She held the radio as if she were trying to figure it out. "Well, goodnight."

"Goodnight."

Mercedes slept on the sofa in the living room that night, and the night after that, and then Mama borrowed a rollaway from the neighbors. I got used to Mercedes pretty quickly, but Mama was transformed. I watched her buzz around the living room, emptying ashtrays, discovering candy wrappers stuffed under chair cushions, removing ink stains from upholstery, never complaining. She plainly loved Mercedes, and that surprised me, because my mother wasn't impetuous about anything, least of all love: until I was eighteen, she hugged me only if one of us was going on a trip, and then it was all business. I knew she loved me, of course, but it was a careful affection: regimented, proper. Looking back, I realize she had started loving Mercedes the first time she read *The Rose in the Garden.* It's not even surprising that she brought Mercedes home: Mama had been looking for her for thirty years.

My mother started cooking complicated breakfasts: waffles, bacon, even tiny steaks. Mercedes was an amazing eater. She ate every dish separately: first eggs, scraping the plate clean, then bacon, and finally potatoes. She drank coffee constantly, and I think she ate caffeine pills in between. She barely slept. I heard the talk-show hosts chatting from the living room all night, and sometimes, Mercedes talked back. "Are you crazy?" she asked. "You must be nuts!" Sometimes at breakfast she told us about the loonies that phoned in: the woman who knew her parakeet understood algebra but just couldn't flap his wings well enough to communicate solutions, the man who was sure that God proved himself in ball-game scores. "O America," she said one morning, piercing the yolk of her fried egg with a fork.

After breakfast, Mama went to work, I went to school, and Mercedes went someplace, she wouldn't say where. Mama thought maybe she had a job, but I pictured her at the library, reading magazines or encyclopedias or comic books.

The Thursday after Mercedes arrived, Mama decided she was going to give us haircuts. She spread newspapers on the kitchen floor and got out her scissors and combs.

"Mercedes first," she said. She had sent Mercedes to wash her hair, and it was still tangled, of course, when she sat down in the kitchen. Mama went at it with a comb. I was at the kitchen table, writing a report on the Boston Tea Party. It was due the next day, and I hadn't even gone to the library.

"You have such beautiful hair," Mama told Mercedes. "All you have to do is take care of it."

"It's a bother."

"Just take care of it. Ruthie wouldn't take care of hers, and I had to cut it all off. Be careful, or I'll do it to you."

Mercedes twisted around at the waist. "Don't." She wrapped her fist around her wet hair.

"I was just kidding. Don't take everything so seriously."

Mercedes turned back carefully. "Just a trim. Just enough to keep it growing."

"You want me to set it, too? I could do it up in little pin curls. My sisters and I used to do each other's hair."

I found that hard to believe. When I saw my mother talk to my aunts, they whispered fiercely about my grandmother. They never smiled.

"Okay . . . curls?" Mercedes sounded dubious.

"A few curls."

Mercedes set her head back and closed her eyes.

"We used to have the cutest hairdos when we were little," said my mother. "You know what we set our hair with? Kotex! The kind that attaches to a belt? We thought it was funny, but really, it was just perfect. Sterile, just the right size, and with little handles to tie."

I always thought my mother told these stories to embarrass me. Now Mercedes frowned, her cheeks getting even pinker. She kept her eyes closed.

"You should see my prom picture," Mama said. "All curls, dyed red. My father's in it—he got dolled up in a suit, because he knew my mother would want a picture of the two of us together." My mother sighed. "I look at that picture, and at the picture of me and Pop at my wedding, and I think: God. There's the right sort of man. There's the man I should've gone home with—not my date, certainly not my husband. My father was kind and smart and a good dancer. Your father—" she shook the comb at me accusingly, "—can't dance a step."

"Don't blame me. Not everybody's father is perfect."

"Be polite—"

"Mine wasn't, either." Mercedes opened one eye, turned it toward me, and closed it again. Then she lit a cigarette without even looking.

"But he wasn't a bad man, right? He encouraged you." Mama started to cut a tangle free.

"He encouraged me."

"My father was gallant. That's the word for him, just gallant. He always knew when to tell us we looked pretty. He owned a woman's clothing store, and he brought us home dresses. He always knew which one would flatter and fit which daughter. He had a genius for people. But he was serious, too. He was a good reader."

"My father was serious," said Mercedes.

"Well, he'd have to be. He was a professor, right?"

Mercedes paused the way she always did when she thought she was going to be fooled into something. "Yes," she said finally. "He taught geography. To this day, I can't locate Italy on the map."

"Anyone can find Italy," I said. "Even I know Italy."

"Not me," said Mercedes.

Mama started snipping at the ends of the hair. "But he encouraged you, you said. He gave you compliments."

"Not really. He didn't insult me. I barely saw him; I dealt with my mother. She gave me all my education. My father was an academic. He was too far away from reality to be ambitious. My mother wanted to be famous."

Mama bit her lip and looked at the back of Mercedes's head, trying not to look too interested, not knowing what to do to keep Mercedes talking.

She didn't have to do anything; Mercedes went on by herself. "He never paid much attention to me. I thought he didn't care about girls at all. My mother once said to me, thank God she found my father, who didn't notice the fact that she wasn't feminine. But once . . . I was sitting with him in his den, typing a paper. I loved typing, still do: if you work hard enough at it, you can be perfect, no mistakes—very satisfying. My father was sitting in his easy chair, reading a book. For some reason I mentioned my cousin Edith in St. Louis. My father looked up; whatever he was about to say was important enough to make him put down his book. 'Now, there's a pretty girl,' he said.

'Stunning, I'd say. Just beautiful. Always has been.' And there I was, just looking at my father. Slack-jawed. Cheated. All those years, pretending it didn't matter. How could he do that to my mother and me? He changed the rules right then, he just changed the rules."

We were quiet. Mama snipped awhile. "You're pretty," she said suddenly. "Mercedes, you're a very pretty lady."

"Mmmm," she said, her eyes still closed. "That's a lie. I mean, it's not like I ever wanted to be. I knew I was no good at it. I could look at Edith and see there was no point even thinking about it. I always wanted to be good at something, the best, so good that other people'd despair at even trying. But there never was anything."

"Very pretty," said my mother, "Beautiful hair, and color—"

"It doesn't matter, anyhow," I said.

Mercedes sat at attention and pointed at me. Her hair pulled out of my mother's fingers. "Bingo," she said. "That's it exactly." She stood up. "Enough. You're finished, aren't you?"

"I thought we were going to set it," said my mother.

"That's silly. A waste of time." Mercedes slipped off the towel that was around her neck and put it on the table. She looked embarrassed. "I'm going to rest."

"Well," said Mama. "I guess you're next, Ruthie."

"Can't we do it tomorrow? I have homework."

"Is it math? Mercedes can help you."

"No I can't," said Mercedes. "I haven't got a head for figures." She left the room, trailing smoke.

"Imagine," said my mother, after a moment. "Do you think that's it? Do you think that's what's done it? She's a genius, a genius, and all those years, just wanting to be pretty. She was famous, she was in the papers. Her future was so bright—"

"I don't think that's it," I said, but what I thought was: answers don't come that easy.

I woke up in the middle of the night, not knowing what time it was. Mercedes still had my radio. I walked to the kitchen to look at the clock and maybe get something to eat.

When I got there, Mercedes was at the table, reading my report where I had left it.

"Hey," I said crossly. I was sleepy and feeling fussy.

"Oh—" She dropped it. "I was just reading—"

"Well, don't. I don't need someone going through, correcting my spelling."

"I wasn't, I wouldn't." She stuttered, panicked. "I was only interested. I don't know anything about the Boston Tea Party."

I took the report off the table and crunched it up angrily. "I know I'm not smart. I don't need someone pointing it out. We all *know* you're a genius, Mercedes."

She looked terrified, as if I was going to hit her or make her speak French. "I'm not," she said. "I'm not at all smart. Please don't think I am."

"I don't know who you think you're fooling. I think it's mean pretending you're stupid when you're not. It's like pretending you're blind or crippled just to get out of stuff."

"Ruthie, Ruthie," she said. "You're smarter than you know."

"Mmmm," I said, doing a dead-on, cruel impression. "That's a lie."

We looked at each other. I shook my head and said, just like mother did sometimes, "You know, I simply don't understand you." It was true. I'm sure she heard it in my voice.

"Oh yes," she said. "That much I do know."

That night I cried in bed, replaying the scene. I was furious with myself, and furious with my mother, and furious with Mercedes. But I knew which one of us was guiltiest, and pinched my thighs and slapped my stomach, rolling in the sheets.

Mercedes disappeared before we got up. Mama was frantic—she took the day off work and drove around the city.

"Did she say anything to you?" she asked me. "Did she give you any hints?"

"No," I said, miserable. "Nothing."

I found a gift from Mercedes on my desk. It was my report, typed neatly, all the spelling and historical mistakes corrected, but without too much ambition. She had read and memorized it all at once—Mama said that she had a photographic memory. Mercedes knew that I wouldn't be too proud to take it if she snuck it in. I was grateful, I admit. I had ruined my only clean copy of it.

She left my mother a copy of *The Rose in the Garden,* with the word *Love* written on the title page. She didn't get around to signing her name. All there was was that one word.

We never heard from her again. Mama scouted the libraries, the grocery stores, the boardinghouses. She took out classified ads in the newspapers, hoping that someone would find her and call us. Whenever we were in the car, looking down driveways and in doorways, if we spotted a small silhouette or a wisp of smoke, my mother slowed down. "That her?" she asked. I always was the one to decide it wasn't. At Christmas time, when she figured that Mercedes would be loneliest, Mama stuck up signs all over downtown that said, "Mercedes, We Miss You.

Come Back For X-Mas. Love, Ellen and Ruthie." Nothing in return.

I turned in that report she wrote for me and got an F. The note at the bottom said: "You know you weren't supposed to get help."

WHAT WE KNOW ABOUT THE LOST AZTEC CHILDREN

THE OLD MAN OPENED our front door just wide enough to stick his head in and peer around like a bashful jack-in-the-box. Then he rested his chin on the doorknob. He was so short he barely had to bend over.

"Hello?" I said.

"Here's to you, boy," he answered, staring at me evenly. The pale gray color of his eyes seemed stingily applied, though his white hair was generous and pumped full of air over his oddly shaped head.

I didn't know what to make of him, and it

looked like the feeling was mutual. He was clearly sizing me up: muddy sneakers, clean otherwise, teen-aged. No danger at all. He finished opening the door and walked in; my mother followed and kicked the door closed behind her.

"Steven," she said to me. "This is your Uncle Plazo."

The rest of him was as odd as his head: a tiny old man dressed in a bright serape, navy pants, and shabby loafers. He was four feet tall, if that, proportioned like a child, but skinny as a parking meter. He gripped an unlit pipe in his teeth.

I held my hand out. "Nice to meet you," I said.

The man took the pipe from his mouth, and with the same hand took mine, so that we both clasped the bowl. He shook my whole arm. "Fucking A," he answered. "Absolutely, absolutely." His voice was excited and boyish.

I laughed; Ma shot me a look.

"We don't use that sort of language, Plazo," she told the man. Then she asked me, "Where are Helen and Carol?"

"Upstairs," I said.

My mother started up the stairs, my unknown Uncle Plazo holding on to a fold of her full skirt. When he and Ma came back down seconds later, my sisters trailed afterward. Ma and Uncle Plazo went into the kitchen; Carol and Helen stood in the doorway, gawking a minute, then came to talk to me.

"Who is he?" asked Carol.

"No idea."

"He's our uncle?" Helen asked.

"I don't think so," I said. "I mean, he could be a great-uncle, but wouldn't we have heard of him?"

"He could be from Tennessee," said Carol. Ma was originally from Nashville, and we always considered it a very exotic place.

"He doesn't have an accent," I said. "It's just an expression, you know, calling an old guy an uncle."

"But didn't you notice?" said Helen.

"Notice what?"

Helen looked carefully at Carol, who at eleven was our youngest, three years younger than me and two younger than Helen. "Well—" Helen said.

"Maybe he's just senile," I said. "He's old."

Helen shook her head. "Betty Snow has a brother like that," she said. "You can tell."

From the kitchen we heard Ma say, "Plazo, could you bring me the bag of rice from the cupboard?"

Apparently, Ma's warning about language impressed the man, because he said now, in stentorian tones, "It would be my greatest pleasure."

We walked to the door of the kitchen. Uncle Plazo was talking about snakes and why he liked them. My mother was just closing the fridge with her foot. She turned to look at us, while Plazo kept on talking.

"We were just wondering—" I said.

"Plazo," Ma said, "is a friend from the circus."

My mother had been a circus performer in the early thirties, years before I was born. This much I knew: she did not walk the high wire or dance in the lion's cage or work under the big top at all. She did not perform in spangles or feathers or a low-cut dress, though sometimes when I was younger I'd imagined her that way. My mother's act consisted of cutting silhouettes, smoking a cigarette, signing her name, loading and firing a gun.

What transformed these simple acts into miracles was that my mother, the Armless Wonder, did them all with her feet.

Some ignorant people say, What a shame, your mother couldn't hold you when you were a baby. But of course she did hold me, the same way she did everything: with her strong legs. I can't remember ever even thinking about it. She nursed me, too, steadying my head in the curve of her sole. Perhaps she tickled my ears with her toes. A baby is not as complicated as a gun, and more forgiving. Ma had me figured out pretty quickly, and my sisters Carol and Helen soon after. When I asked my father about the circus, he'd just shrug. He was a doctor, and dispensed advice, not information. My mother almost never spoke of her circus career.

I did not dream about my mother's life in the circus. I was not a dreamer—I just made certain assumptions, had pictured her with exotic men in black suits or canary-yellow leotards. It didn't occur to me that my mother had spent her time in the Ten-in-One, the sideshow, and that meant a different sort of company.

At dinnertime, my father held Uncle Plazo's chair for him, like a suitor. Plazo climbed into it elaborately, first hands, then knees, finally turning to sit down, though he wasn't so short he'd have to do it that way. My father had not prepared for this approach, and Plazo was still two feet from the table. Dad slid the chair and Plazo in with ease.

Uncle Plazo sat next to me. My mother had given him some of my old clothing to wear—a pair of blue jeans and a plaid flannel shirt—and he made them look small and precious. His silver hair stuck straight up in back.

"We used to be the Lost Aztec Children," he said to me.

I smiled at him, unsure of how to answer.

"That's right," he said. "See the amazing Lost Children of Ancient Me-hico, see the Lost Aztec Children, they're amazing, they're the Lost Children, Plazo and Zleeno. They're not like you and me, they're from—"

"Plazo worked right next to me in the circus," said Ma.

"That's right," said Plazo. He pushed his food around the plate.

My father sat at the head of the table. Now he did not even seem to notice Uncle Plazo; it was as if this strange small man was just one of the children's friends, brought home for a meal.

Carol lifted up the serving plate. "Would you like some more chicken, Uncle Plazo?"

"Sure thing," he said. "I love chicken. I eat it whenever I get a chance. Chicken's my favorite."

"Plazo," said Ma. "You still have some chicken on your plate."

"That's because it's good," he said. "You can never have too much chicken."

"Why don't you finish what's on your plate, and then if you're still want it, you can have some more."

"We won't let you go hungry," said my father.

"I'm never hungry," said Uncle Plazo. He picked up a carrot and weighed it in his palm. "I used to be hungry all the time, but now I'm not, not since all that trouble." He looked at me. "My brother died on me, I don't know why."

"That's too bad," I said.

"It is too bad, it really is. Died on me two hundred seventy-three days ago. He died of old age, that's what they told me, but he was younger than me, he was one year and thirty days younger. I miss him."

"Of course you do," said Ma. Uncle Plazo was looking at his plate; his mouth looked worried that it'd run out of things to say.

"It's sad to lose a brother," Dad said.

"Corrine knew my brother," said Uncle Plazo. "You knew my brother, right, Corrine? We were the Lost Aztec Children."

"Where are you from?" I asked.

"From the jungles of Aztec," he said. "From the jungles of ancient Me-hico."

"You don't look Mexican," I said.

"I'm not," said Uncle Plazo.

"Where were you *born*?" asked Carol.

"Who cares?" he said. "Waltham, Massachusetts." He pushed his plate away and began to fill his pipe. "I was born there, but I'm not from there. I'm from the jungle, I'm the missing link."

"What did you do in the circus?" I asked.

"I was the Lost Aztec Children."

"But did you do an act?" I asked. "Did you sing or lift things?"

He was quiet for a minute, thinking. "I didn't talk," he said finally. "They paid me a nickel a day not to talk."

That night, in his den, my father told us Uncle Plazo's story. Plazo's real name was Hiram, but he'd been called Plazo so long it was all he answered to. He'd grown up in the circus with his brother, had traveled for sixty years before the two of them retired to Boston, to a tiny one-room apartment. But the brother died, and either he'd been the one in charge or the two of them had managed—just managed—together. The neighbors found Plazo hiding in one bed, his brother dead in the other. He'd given the neighbors our number.

"I don't understand," I said. "People paid money to see two little retarded men?"

My father pulled at his ear and didn't look at me. "People will pay to see anything," he said, "if somebody tells them it's worth the money. Now he's a guest. Steven," he said. "I want you to watch out for him."

"Why me?" I complained. I had my own things to do; I didn't want to hang around the Lost Aztec Child.

"You're older," he said, "and I just think he'd be more comfortable around you. I'm asking you a favor, all right?"

"Okay," I said.

My father must have known that Uncle Plazo would be frightened of Helen and Carol—called them only "those girls"—and the feeling was mutual. "He's creepy," said Carol. "His eyes are spooky." But he took to me. When I came home from school the day after his arrival, he was waiting by the front door.

"Stevie boy, Stevie," he said.

He had a pile of pictures in his lap. Some of them were quite old, probably acquired when he first started traveling. They just looked like ordinary old photographs, the sort that any member of late nineteenth-century society might pose for: the backgrounds were painted; there was usually one piece of elegant furniture. A bearded lady stood behind her seated husband, their young son leaning on the arm of the chair. The Skeleton Dude, in tight ribbed pants, a tailcoat, a monocle, conferred with his manservant. An albino with hair that stood in a halo around his head was captioned The Ambassador from Mars. An armless woman—not my mother—held a pen between her toes.

"This one's us," Uncle Plazo said, handing me a cardboard-backed photo. In it, two little men who looked identical stood on either side of a much taller, bearded man. I couldn't tell which one was Plazo; they certainly did look like odd children. Both were dressed in tunics decorated with cut-out suns; both held their hands in front of them, as if they were about to sing. Their hair was long and straight, and they sported goatees. The man in the center looked like a biblical prophet or a school principal, I couldn't decide which.

"Who's the guy in the middle?" I asked.

"He's dead," said Uncle Plazo. "He's long dead and he's good riddance. I don't care about him a bit. See, this is Zleeno—" he pointed to the Aztec Child on the left, "—and this is me. This is a long time ago, Stevie boy, before you were born."

I studied the photo awhile, to make it seem like I was interested in it. Pasted to the back was a little pamphlet, titled, "What We Know About Plazo and Zleeno, the Lost Aztec Children." The pages were crumpling at the edges. A woodcut decorated the front: Plazo and Zleeno in the wild, with several men in suits trying to catch them with nets.

"Our true history," said Uncle Plazo.

I opened the booklet and read, "Scientific men who have studied the Lost Aztec Children believe they are neither idiots, nor *lusus naturae*, but the solitary remaining members of a now forgotten race. Undersized and ferocious, they hold no intercourse with the civilized tribes, and can kill a tiger with their bare hands."

I looked at Uncle Plazo. He blinked rapidly and smiled.

I flipped through the rest of the pile. After a while the formal photographs turned to postcards, some with several poses of the performer and banner captions across them. The Seal Boy, with flippers instead of arms and legs; the Tattooed Beauty; a pair of angry Siamese twins. I began to feel relieved that we had ended up with only this fast-talking old man.

Finally, I hit one of Ma. She held a cigarette between her toes, elegantly, like a movie star. Her clothing was conservative and pretty, free of the glitz I'd always imagined: she wore just a full skirt and a blouse, a few silk flowers at the throat. Her makeup had been glamorously applied, and though I knew from the date on the back that she was only sixteen, I couldn't believe it. I had never seen a picture of my mother before her marriage; I had never even seen a picture of her without my father. We had plenty of the two of them, and in these photographs Dad was always touching Ma: an arm around her waist, a hand on the back of her neck. In their wedding photo, he stood behind her, both arms around her as if his limbs were just another asset that they now shared.

But looking at her by herself, I saw how beautiful my mother was then, and still, and how you had to look at what was holding the cigarette to realize it was a foot and not the expected hand, and how she made hands seem like an unfashionable waste of time.

"Most beautiful armless girl in the world," said Uncle Plazo. Even at thirteen I was rather touched. Then he said, "She can do anything, she can wind a watch, she can paint a picture, she can fire a gun," and I realized he was repeating my mother's pitch. But when I looked at him, his face was fond and thoughtful.

The next day, we took Uncle Plazo to the grocery store. He offered to drag the little red wagon we always used when my father was unable to drive us. My mother had to slow down her usual straight-ahead stride: Uncle Plazo walked like a wind-up toy, moving quickly but not efficiently. He was easily impressed by the cars that drove past; by strangers, street signs, movie marquees; by radios playing from windows. He might as well have been from the jungles of ancient Mexico, so unaccustomed did he seem to everyday suburban life.

The sides of Ma's body were expressive, and useful, and now she caressed us with a hip to show she was interested, but in a hurry. She'd carefully sewn up the sleeves of her dress, to show neither skin nor loose flapping fabric. I imagined she'd always done that; she'd been born without arms. My father explained to me that my mother's mother had probably been sick during her pregnancy, a virus. It could have been so small she'd never even noticed she was ill.

Inside the store, Plazo seemed amazed by the shopping carts, and pushed ours, looking even shorter behind it since he had to reach up; I stuck the little red wagon sideways inside the basket. "Oranges," he said, admiring a pyramid of them. "Will you look at that? Will you just look at those oranges?"

"Would you like an orange?" Ma asked.

"Hell no," said Uncle Plazo. "Can't stand the things. Zleeno liked 'em, but not me. Look." He pointed to an abandoned bottle nestled in the bananas, and he carefully read off the label, "*Salad* dressing." He laughed.

As we went through the store, it became increasingly obvious that his wonder was to a large extent politeness. "What do you know," he said. "Bacon. Ham."

"What would you like to eat?" Ma asked.

"Oh, nothing for me," he said. "But thank you for your concern."

When we checked out, Ma said, "Do you want to pay, Plazo? Steve, pull out my wallet for Uncle Plazo."

I fished out her wallet from her skirt pocket and handed it to him. He seemed alarmed at the sight of the money. The girl rang up our groceries.

"That'll be eleven eighty-two, please," she said.

Uncle Plazo pulled out a handful of bills and offered them. She smiled at him.

"You've given me too much," she said.

"Really?" He sounded delighted, as if he had just discovered in himself a great capacity for kindness.

The clerk wrinkled her nose and laughed. "New in town, aren't you," she said.

"Plazo is visiting us," Ma said.

"Where from?" the girl asked. "Mars?" She handed Uncle Plazo the change.

"No, not from Mars," he told her. "I once knew a man from Mars."

"Oh, did you now," she said. "That isn't hard to believe."

"Come on," said Ma. "Let's get going."

"He has unbelievable strength," said Uncle Plazo, as usual slipping into the present tense of the bally. "The man from Mars can lift two ordinary earth men."

"Uh-huh," said the girl. "I'm sure he can."

Ma was standing by the door. "Come on, men," she said.

I lifted the grocery bags off the counter into the red wagon and offered the handle to Uncle Plazo.

"The man from Mars," he said to me outside, "was from Kentucky. I always liked him."

* * *

After our trip to the grocery store, Uncle Plazo wanted to take walks all the time. When I got home from school, he was waiting for me, dressed in the blue jeans and plaid shirt he now lived in: the world's smallest lumberjack. Sometimes he wore his serape, too, even though it was June and warm. He was always cold, as if he really believed he was from a tropical climate.

"You know—" he said, stepping out into the street.

I put my hand on his shoulder. "Not yet," I said. "There's a car coming. We'll wait."

He nodded. "I always thought Zleeno would make it to a hundred. Didn't you?"

"I didn't know him." The car passed and we started across.

"But didn't you think he would? Make it to a hundred?"

"I guess," I said. "A hundred's pretty old."

"It is pretty old," he said. "But it's possible. Plenty of people make it to that age, just doing nothing."

We turned the corner and started past the high school. A gang of tough kids was playing on the baseball diamond.

"Hey!" they yelled. "Stop!"

One solitary boy came running up to us. He was a short, fat kid; the rims of his nostrils were caked with old blood.

"Where are you going," he said. He punched me on the arm. It hurt, but rubbing it would seem cowardly, so I didn't.

"We're just walking," I said. "That any crime?"

"Who are you," he said to Uncle Plazo. "The runt of the litter?"

"Maybe so," said Uncle Plazo. "But you're sure not a runt, not you."

The fat boy blushed. His friends clung to the backstop of the baseball diamond.

"Where did you come from?" he asked. "Mars?"

Uncle Plazo cackled. "Everybody around here thinks I'm from Mars." He shook his head. "Nope."

"Leave him alone," I said. "He's just a harmless old guy."

"Who are you, his keeper?" The boy scratched his stomach.

I did not particularly want to choose between the tough kids and Plazo. Still, I knew I had a duty toward Plazo, and so I said, "He's my uncle. Push off."

The boy started to say something, but changed his mind. "Ugly creeps," he said, and he spit at me, but missed. Then he ran back to his friends.

"Yeah!" they yelled as we walked away. "You better go!"

We walked to the end of the block in silence. Uncle Plazo crossed his hands beneath his serape and held on to his skinny elbows. Finally, he said, "I've never been in a place like this all my life."

The school year came to an end, my last year at the middle school. Uncle Plazo had been with us a month. In the fall I'd go on to the high school, where the rough kids hung out, but for now I was a big kid in my own right. I didn't want to spend every afternoon walking with Plazo.

Ma decided Uncle Plazo was allowed to take a walk by himself, as long as he didn't go off the block.

"Just keep going around, and soon enough you'll be home," said Ma. She had my father hang a birdhouse in the front yard as a landmark.

"Okay," said Uncle Plazo. He carried a compass that somebody had given him, and sometimes when I got home I'd see him coming the other way, looking intently at his compass. Sometimes, he'd walk right past the house. Usually a neighborhood kid or two would be trailing him.

"It's probably dinnertime," I'd tell him, and he'd look up and smile. The kids would scatter. I wanted to call out to them. "Not my uncle!" I imagined shouting. But my parents trusted me to do the right thing, so Uncle Plazo and I went up the walk and into the house together.

"Stompy was a great guy," said Uncle Plazo. He was sitting at the kitchen table, cross-legged on the chair. "He died too, I guess. Do you remember how, Corrine?"

"Who?" asked my mother. She was sitting on the tall stool that brought her legs up to counter level so she could work with her feet; she'd kicked off her slippers and was chopping celery.

"Stompy, Stompy, you know."

"Before my time or after it," she said. "Steve, will you wash the green beans for me?"

"How about Madeline? The sword swallower? Remember, Corrine?"

"Her I remember," said Ma. "She scared me. The tall woman?"

"No, not her, the Madeline before. The tall woman wasn't Madeline, we just called her that after the first one."

"Right," said my mother. She shook her head.

"Those were great days," said Uncle Plazo. He had a piece of cake my mother had given him; he mashed it with his fork.

"Oh," said my mother. "I guess."

"You didn't like them? You didn't think they were great days?"

"I was just a child, Plazo," she said. She turned on her stool to face him. "I was twenty when I left."

"A child?" he said. He stared at her, as if, having spent so many years being one of the Lost Aztec Children, he thought that child was a job, not a stage of life.

"I was only a teenager, Plazo," my mother said. "I was easily scared."

"No, no," said Plazo. "No, not really?"

Ma smiled apologetically.

Plazo uncrossed his legs and set his heels on the chair's edge. "I grew up there," he said thoughtfully.

"I know you did," she said.

I don't know what he thought "there" was, whether he meant a certain time or the accumulation of all the places he had stayed. He tilted his head as if he were trying to see something.

"But scared," said Uncle Plazo. "Sure, I can picture it. I can picture being scared."

"Weren't you ever?" my mother asked. "Isn't this better?"

Uncle Plazo scratched his nose. I could see him decide not to answer.

I thought Uncle Plazo regretted being with us. Back in Boston, where he had lived with his brother, he'd probably found my mother's address and thought: she's good folk, she's like me. He wanted to be with people he could talk about his life with, to stay on with the circus in any little way he could. In this, I thought, he'd be like any man forced into retirement. But here he was in the suburbs of Cleveland, with an absolutely ordinary family.

Because the fact is we were ordinary. If somebody asked what was different, I might say, well perhaps my mother needed me a little more than most mothers. It isn't true, though: that I felt especially needed was part of her talent. Her only flamboyances were a fondness for capes and slippers and a dislike of stockings, all for practical reasons. The only thing she couldn't do was—I want to say play piano, rock-climb, swim—but though I never saw her do these things, I'm not sure she couldn't have. She couldn't turn a cartwheel; she couldn't jump rope by herself. But how many mothers can? She could hold the rope for my sisters, play jacks with them, could braid their hair; she could type and open jars and button my coat. My mother's handicap, if that's the dull word we are using, had nothing to do with me, or with anybody but herself. Everything in our life seemed usual, normal, average—even, I thought sometimes, boring.

That now included Uncle Plazo. He might have seemed interesting at first, but that wore off quick. The exoticness that people had paid to gawk at for so long was just a story that somebody had made up. My father was right: you could make anybody amazing just by insisting they were. Away from the pitchman, Uncle Plazo was powerless. The neighborhood kids were just listening to their own pitch, their own stories on where he came from and what he meant.

Uncle Plazo got restless as fall approached. He spoke of his brother more and more, things that his brother did. It was as if Zleeno were a fictional character loosely based on him; he shook his head and laughed admiringly, as if he had never done those things himself: talked back of the bally with the Skeleton Dude, who had taught the Lost Aztec Children some impeccable manners and some cusswords; looked up at a bannerline with his own picture on it; ridden across country on a train.

When it rained, Uncle Plazo walked through the house, up the stairs, down them. He'd appear for dinner with cobwebs in his hair or with a bug he'd found in the basement; one time, he found one of the snakes he so loved and presented it to Ma. The neighbors complained that he walked through their yards and yelled things at their dogs. Once, he walked in followed by our cat, who was growling. The cat and Plazo did not get along at the best of times, but we had never before seen the cat openly complain.

"Do you know what that cat did?" said Uncle Plazo. "She was going to kill a mouse."

"That's the reason we have her," said Ma.

"To kill mice? You have a cat so it can kill mice? Look—" he said, and he opened his hand. A mouse balanced on his palm for just a minute, then sprang out of it, hit the floor, and ran into the corner, followed by the cat. Ma screamed; so did I.

"No!" yelled Plazo. "That cat's going to do it again! She's going to kill that mouse!" He ran after the cat, who now had the mouse in her mouth and growled through her mouthful. I quickly got to the back door to let it out.

"I don't want this cat to kill that mouse," said Uncle Plazo as the cat bellied out the door. He wrung his hands; he looked like he was going to cry.

Ma sat down at the kitchen table. "Come here, Plazo," she said. He did, and she put a foot on his leg, behind his knee. "A cat has to kill a mouse; that's its nature. You've seen that before."

"Just because I see something doesn't mean I like it. I've seen a million things, a million things, and I didn't like some of them, not a bit."

Ma took a deep breath. "But the cat helps us keep our house clean. Mice are dirty, and the cat cleans them up."

"Clean's not so great," he said, stepping away from Ma's leg. "Depends on how you get clean."

My parents had hushed conversations about him. One night, I snuck out of bed to listen; I assumed they were making plans to send him off somewhere. But what I overheard that night was, *YMCA* and *swimming lessons* and *church if he wanted.*

"Roller skating," Dad said suddenly, as if it were a solution he'd been looking for all his life.

Ma laughed. "Oh, maybe," she said. "Maybe. But somehow I doubt it."

My parents finally decided on something the whole family could help with. "He can read," Ma told us. "Do you know what it means that he's learned how?"

I shrugged. We were sorting through some of our old books, trying to find something that would turn Uncle Plazo into a reader.

"I could read when I was three," said Carol, though this was an exaggeration.

"That's because you had an older brother and sister to teach you," said Ma. She was looking at *The Little Engine That Could.* Some smiling fruit beamed up at her from the page. "There's no reason he ever needed to know how. Nobody ever taught him. He picked it up himself."

"He just reads signs," I said. "Just one or two words at a time."

"That's how everyone starts. One word at a time." She flipped the book open with her toe. "He's spent enough time on trains in his life. Maybe he'd like this."

But Plazo didn't want to read; he said he held no truck with books. He was sitting in the kitchen with the radio on, some housekeeping show.

"I don't know what's to become of me," he told Ma, though he was smiling.

She didn't say anything, just shook her head.

Plazo stood up and pulled his compass out of his pocket. "Going for a walk," he said.

"Be back soon," said Ma.

"Be back soon," he answered.

When the door closed, Ma said, "Oh dear. Now what?"

"Well," I said. "It could be worse. We could have to take care of the seal boy."

Ma turned and stared at me. "What's your point?"

"I dunno," I said. I wasn't used to my mother being angry; she almost never was. "Just—at least he's only going through the neighbors' yards on two feet, not on all fours and his stomach. We could have done worse than a dummy."

Ma walked over to me deliberately, hooked one leg around both of mine, and knocked me to the floor. My head hit the fridge.

"See how you like being that close to the ground," she said.

I started to get up, but she put a foot on my chest and held me there.

"See how you like not being able to stand up."

Her leg was strong, and I didn't fight it. "I'm sorry," I said.

"You're pretty sorry, yeah. You're not such a prize yourself, you know. Listen: anybody who wants to stay with us can, if I say they can." She shook her head sadly. "So, Steven," she asked. "What do you say about me, when I'm not around?"

I shook my head in horror. "Nothing—"

"How do I know that?" She looked defeated, exhausted.

"Until five seconds ago I didn't know you were this hateful." Her voice was quiet, and I could tell that she didn't believe what she was saying. It was a punishment, one that worked.

Carol and Helen were huddled in the doorway. I put my hand on Ma's ankle but couldn't say anything.

"I'm just disgusted with you," she said. She gave me a final shove with her foot, then turned around and left the room. Carol and Helen both burst into tears, as if Ma's line were their cue.

I stayed on the floor in the kitchen for a while, away from my mother. I could feel the print of her foot on my chest, the hill of her ankle where it had rushed past my palm. Finally, I stood up and went to the hall and watched her in the living room. She kept peering through the window, looking for Plazo.

"Do you want me to go find him?" I asked.

"No," she said. "We'll give him a little more time." She sat down in the easy chair. "Will you come here?"

I walked over to her. "I never say anything about you," I said. "Nobody ever does. I'd kill anybody who did."

Ma put one foot on my shoulder, then pulled me toward her in an embrace.

"But I have a pretty face," she said.

I just looked at her. I was wearing shorts, and my shins were against the edge of the chair; the rough upholstery dug into my skin. I knew that one of my sisters would say something: "Of course you're pretty, Ma." They would touch her face and suggest playing with her makeup, trying on hats. I said nothing.

"People can forget about me," she said. "If we sit down and talk, people can forget there's anything different about me at all. It's what they want to do. I can see it every time I meet somebody. They think: God, let me forget about what's wrong with this woman."

"There's nothing wrong with you," I said.

My mother shook her head. "They want to forget about me, and I want them to forget." Her feet were on my calves. "But is that fair?" she said. "Why should I want them to?"

"Because it doesn't make any difference," I said.

"Oh yes," she said. "It does."

And at that moment I realized: My mother had let us forget it was a gift she'd always given us. Somehow, she'd let us think she'd forgotten, too.

"You have a beautiful face," I told her.

She let her feet drop to the ground, and her beautiful face was full of doubt.

Uncle Plazo's strangeness wore thin on the neighborhood kids soon enough, and they left him alone. Acts that get old lose their luster. The ambassador from Mars, sliding into his seventies, can comb down his now-thinning hair, don shaded glasses, and just look like any pale elderly man. Giants shrink; the fat lady dies young. The sword swallower poisons himself swallowing a neon tube that bursts in his stomach.

These are all stories Uncle Plazo told me once he found out that his memories interested me, if not my mother. Those who don't die fall out of fashion or tire of the life or find a new twist: the snake charmer gets tattooed; the Texas Giant and the half-lady become the World's Strangest Married Couple. And Uncle Plazo, ex-wild man, ex-child, ex-brother, became simply one more confused old guy in Ohio, solo now, smaller than most, perhaps lost for good. But less scared, I think, never disappointed with where his life ended up, happy that he had a new attraction. The Man Who Never Forgets. The Fantastic Ohio Fabulist. Maybe only to me, but I'd like to think I was enough.

He lived with us two more years, the rest of his life. When he died, my mother tracked down some relatives out East, who had dim memories but no interest in their cousin. One sent a letter telling us that Plazo, she thought, must have been about eighty—which was about fifteen years older than we'd guessed.

Ma arranged for him to be buried near us and paid to get his brother—whose name was Barney—moved from his unmarked grave to our town.

"I just want to show that they're not freaks," Ma had told the Massachusetts cousins. "I'm sure you'd do the same if you were able."

The funeral was a quiet affair. My mother wore a black scarf around her head and a black sleeveless dress. It was perhaps not quite appropriate for the occasion, and she for once did not sew the sleeves closed. Her shoulders were not the smooth, doll-like surfaces you might imagine; there was a soft extra curve to them, and a few small fingers that did not move.

Zleeno and Plazo, the Lost Aztec Children, were buried under a stone that says:

GOOD MEN.
HIRAM CAULKEY 1868–1953
BARNEY CAULKEY 1869–1951

Ma slipped her foot from her black shoe and threw the first dirt in.

JUNE

I MOVED TO WATERTOWN, Massachusetts, with one thousand boxes and my parents. We arrived one summer day, having driven across country for educational purposes; the boxes came the next morning, with only some broken china as souvenirs. All those cartons were a formidable sight, and at dinnertime we hid out at the Amazing Chinese Restaurant, down the street.

It was summer, and when we got home from dinner we had to open all the windows: they seemed as unused to the sticky heat as we were, had swelled in their frames and needed to be hit at and spoken to. My parents went from room to room, slamming the windows and peeking in boxes for fans. Outside, some teenage boys fixed cars and revved engines; a few dogs barked. Then we heard a woman's voice calling her children.

"June!" she yelled. "Jill! Johnny!" When she got no answer, she screamed, "June! Get your fucking ass home right now!"

My father smiled; my mother looked stunned.

"We need to find some fans," she said quietly.

"I mean it!" the woman across the street yelled. "Don't pull this shit! One. Two—" and then a girl's voice, too close not to have heard all this time, answered, "Okay, okay."

I had loved Portland. It was a clean city, with weather so delicate that at night you had to look at the streetlights to tell whether it was raining or snowing. Everything was heavier near Boston: air, accents, women. Even the candy was difficult, sugary capsules that caked your teeth, aggressive licorice or cinnamon or even coffee; jawbreakers that jacked my ten-year-old mouth wide open; caramel wrapped around clots of powdered sugar. In Oregon, I had eaten sweets from the Japanese fruit market, candy so willing to be consumed that even the rice-paper wrapper dissolved on my tongue.

I couldn't make sense of the ways things worked in our new neighborhood. Ours was the only single-family house on a street of duplexes; I couldn't imagine two families living under one roof. Mac's Smoke Shop, where I bought my candy, also sold work pants, dusty canned goods, and, I was later to find out, illegal numbers. There was a bar next door to Mac's, a doughnut shop, a Woolworth's, and nearby the wide turnpike, noisy as an ocean. The buildings were jammed close at either side, like heavy traffic. My first morning there, I walked to the bridge that ran over the Pike and looked down, as if I were examining some raucous new animal life.

We'd been there four days when my father opened the door to have a cigarette (by order of me, he wasn't allowed to smoke in the house), and said, "Oho."

"None of your doorbells work," said a girl's voice.

"Well, thank you for bringing that to our attention," Dad said. I stood in the hall behind him and couldn't see past.

"Can the girl come out to play?" said the voice.

"Ask yourself." My father stepped out, eager for his smoke. "Phoebe? For you."

The girl on our porch had sandy, boy-cut hair and store-bought terry-cloth rompers. She was bigger than me, though probably not older.

"You play kickball?" she asked.

"Sure," I said, my first lie in a new state.

"I'm June. I live over there." She pointed at the huge lime green house across the street. Instead of a front lawn, it had a patch of concrete painted with yellow lines, like a parking lot.

"You got brothers and sisters?" she asked.

I told her no.

"Lucky." She brushed her hair to the side and gave me a world-weary look. "I got about a ton."

Our houses were at the elbow of an L-shaped street, and we played right out in the middle of it. I understood the basic rules of kickball, since they were the same as the baseball games my father had made me watch in preparation for the Red Sox. Because only two of us were playing, June used a complicated system of invisible runners. Her runners were always bringing in points; mine seemed to start running and then make a break for freedom down the street. She creamed me, then decided she liked me.

June had only three brothers and sisters—an older, sullen brother named Jeff, and the twins, Johnny and Jilly, who were nine. She had other things I lacked: cowlicks, cavities, Barbie dolls, a number of relatives who lived with her, a record player and some glossy 45s, and her period. I, she explained to me, had these advantages: long hair, a resident father, my own room. June told me I was lucky in a voice that made me sure I was not.

After kickball, we wandered down to the grocery store parking lot at the end of the street. From half a block away, we heard: "JUNE GET YOUR FUCKING ASS HOME RIGHT NOW!"

I looked at her wide-eyed, though I recognized the voice—I'd heard it every night since we'd been there.

"My mother," June explained. "Gotta go."

"Glad you found a friend," my mother said to me that night, our fifth at the Amazing Chinese Restaurant; we hadn't found the kitchenware yet. "She in your grade at school?"

"I guess," I said. June thrilled me, in the way that a bully who befriends you can. Other things didn't sit as well. She and her immediate family lived in the downstairs of their duplex, with her mother's folks upstairs and aunts and uncles on both floors. Terry, June's mother, scared me. I had finally met her close up when we walked back from the lot. She was doughy fat, slack-skinned and slack-voiced from all the cigarettes she smoked. "New kid," she'd said upon our meeting. "There goes the neighborhood." ("She's kidding," June had to tell me.) Terry's slick flowered shirt gapped over her stomach. I was a precocious child, a terrible prude: the fact that Terry was a mother, like my mother was, terrified and fascinated me.

"Well, Phoebe," said my father, raising a can of beer, "here's to our new town." My mother lifted her Coke; I hoisted my ginger ale. The sound of the three full cans meeting was dull and disappointing.

June and I spent some days in the grocery store parking lot. She showed me how to place shopping carts near the cement parking blocks so that the semis that delivered food might back into them and knock the baskets off the wheels. Sometimes it worked. We'd try to turn them into go-carts: they didn't steer, they were uncomfortable, but they rolled and the store didn't mind if we took them. Later, we'd walk back and play in the street in front of our houses. We loved it when a confused car would come the wrong way down our one-way street: we jumped on the curb and screamed, "ONE WAY," at the top of our lungs, happy we knew something they didn't.

Playing in the street, my mother told me, was dangerous. I knew that, but the whole neighborhood seemed dangerous; I felt like I needed to learn a new set of rules. Reckless bravery. So as the cars drove by, I rested only my heels on the curb and dangled my toes in the street, the way June did; sometimes I threw rocks at passing hubcaps; I leapt off June's front porch and hit the pavement on my knees. None of this seemed quite brave enough. So one afternoon at the end of the summer, I followed June into her house for the first time.

The front room was dark; I could smell old smoke and dirty

children. A clock shaped like the sun hung over the beat-up sofa; the coffee table was covered with magazines and crumpled tissues. I heard Terry, June's mother, cough from somewhere deep in the house.

"Ma's got polyps in her throat," said June. I nodded.

One of the doors opened, and a huge woman dressed in men's pajamas stepped out. Her blond hair was kept back with two rubber bands and a battery of bobby pins. I'd seen her before, sitting out on the porch: she was Terry's youngest sister, June's aunt. I knew from June's stories that Annette was mean to the bone, if she had any bones, and looking at her, it was hard to believe she did. Her skin looked packed tight with dense, explosive fat; it shone as if it were being strained to its limits.

"Don't be playin' in here," she said.

"It's my house, too," said June.

The woman blinked. "What did I just say?"

"I'm allowed, An*nette,*" said June.

Annette grabbed June by the arm. "Don't be a shithead," she told June. "And don't bring your shithead friends around." Then she pinched me on the arm.

I considered running. Instead, I said, "See you later, June," and walked out casually.

"They're a very unhappy family," my mother told me when I complained that night. "You should feel sorry for them." My mother believed in liking most people and pitying the rest, which is fine if you've the temperament for it. I didn't.

Neither did my father. He advised me to ignore Annette or to stop playing with June if it bothered me that much or to counter with comebacks he concocted for me. "Tell her, You're hysterical, but looks aren't everything," he said helpfully. Now that I'd been inside June's house, she invited me all the time, and Annette was always there, always angry. One night when I came home particularly upset, Dad offered to talk to Annette, if I thought that would help. I pictured my father going over there, armed with his list of insults, and refused.

I never wanted to go back inside the house, but I knew I had to. The only thing worse than being frightened of doing something is trying it once and giving up for fear.

Annette had a sullen boyfriend named Brian, and when he was around she quieted a bit; the bite went out of her swears, and she stuck her leg out to trip me so lazily when I went by that I was able to dodge it. Brian rarely spoke. He spent of lot of time fixing cars out front, usually with crowbars and hammers. "He's handsome," June said, but all I could see were his pimples, his leather vest, his black feathered hair. I thought of what my father said when he first noticed him: There goes the Neighbor Hood.

My father stood on the front porch, staring at the car. "Who the hell would do this?" Someone had pulled the metal trim off all around and left it attached only at the edges. It hung off like peeled bark. The same someone was terrorizing the neighborhood. It had started as what seemed to be early Halloween mischief—egged cars, garbage strewn on doorsteps—but had lingered and turned malicious.

The neighborhood terrorism enraged my father, who assumed that it was one of the Friel boys, Jeff or Johnny. Dad tested theories on me at dinnertime: Since June was my friend, he thought I'd have some inside information.

"It has to be a boy," he said, "since he instinctively goes for cars. And it has to be a kid, since it's all so unimaginative."

"Could be." I assumed Annette had to be the cause of such plain meanness. Or maybe Johnny, who even his own mother called a rotten fucker. This wasn't so much an insult as a scientific classification. But my father was right; I was a girl, and I wasn't interested in vandalism—my own or somebody else's.

"I have a secret," June said to me one day.

She was wearing a midriff top, and absentmindedly scratched her belly with a box of lemon drops. At any moment she was going to drop it into the pocket of her shorts. Then I was supposed to do the same thing: this was a lesson.

I shushed her. I didn't know how to shoplift, but it did seem to me it should be done in silence.

"Don't you want to know what it is?"

I did, of course, but I was sure the old woman behind the counter was going to catch me any minute. She'd already accused me of stealing once, when I hadn't been, which is why I felt it was okay to do it now. But even the candy at Mac's was dusty and unappealing.

"Phoebe," said June.

"What?" I hissed. "What is it." I started to study the candy rack, three graduated shelves. The candy on the bottom was a nickel a piece, six for a quarter; the second, a dime, three for a quarter; the top, fifteen cents, two for a quarter. I suddenly felt great sorrow at the idea of stealing any of it, it seemed so cheap.

"You know my Aunt Annette?"

"Like I could miss her."

June dropped the candy into her pocket; it hit bottom with a rattle. "She's not really my aunt."

"What is she, the family gorilla?" I fingered a package of Bull's-eyes, which I hated.

"She's really my sister."

"What?" In my limited understanding of how a family worked—and it was changing all the time—I didn't understand how this was possible.

"Ma had her when she was fifteen before she got married and Nana took her over."

"Why doesn't her name start with J, then?" I asked. This seemed like impeccable logic, but June just grabbed some licorice.

"Let's go," I said.

"No. You have to. You said you would."

I looked at the candy again. "No."

"You girls gonna buy anything?" The old woman leaned over the edge. "Hey," she said to me. "Din't I just kick you outa here?"

"No," I said.

"Yeah I did."

"So anyway," said June. "Like I was telling you—"

"You girls get outa here," said the woman. "I know your mothers. I'm gonna tell them."

" 'Scuse *us,*" said June. "So, do you believe me?"

"About what?" I said, sidling to the door.

June grabbed my arm. "What I just told you," she said. "You have to tell me before we leave."

"I'm countin'," said the woman. "One. Two—"

"Yes!" I yelled. "I believe you! Whatever you said!"

June dropped my arm. "That's not the secret, anyway. That's not the *real* secret."

We pushed open the heavy glass door and let in Ghost, the dog who lived at Mac's.

"What is it, then?"

June was already sucking on a Fireball. "Wha'?"

"The secret," I said.

She shrugged. I knew she wouldn't tell me now; I'd failed a test. She tossed the box of lemon drops in the air and caught it. "Your mother hates it here," she said.

"I know."

"Betcha she's gonna leave."

"We might leave," I offered. "I think we might move back."

"No," said June. "I mean, just your mother. She might leave you and your dad. Ma's betting on it."

I felt outraged at the idea that June thought my mother was so fickle she'd choose the Pacific Ocean over me. It scared me, too, since some nights I myself dreamed about hitchhiking back to Oregon and throwing myself on the mercy of my quiet bread-baking ex-neighbors. Besides, Terry had said this? She was stupid, she had no right to talk about me and my parents.

"Your mother's fat," I said.

"So?" said June. The Fireball in her mouth was turning her lips pink. The lemon drops shimmied and clacked in their box as she flipped the box, higher each toss.

"You don't know anything about anything," I said.

June laughed. "Look who's talking, dummy."

The vandalism continued, got worse. Somebody scratched swear words into the paint of all the cars in the neighborhood, then turned their interests on the houses, smashed windows and snapped pickets off fences. Dad was right. It was uninspired criminal activity, notable only for its absolute democracy. My father started getting up in the middle of the night to smoke on the porch.

"Just keeping a lookout," he said.

Meanwhile, someone was beating up June, too. It started with bruises on the pale skin of her upper arms, which made me feel, I'm sorry to say, good—I had the same marks bestowed on me by Annette and by June herself when I beat her at a board game. One day, though, she had a black eye; another, a split lip.

"What happened," I asked.

"You know," she said. Such an answer always stopped me, because I felt I should know; I had once been smart and known things. Now I didn't.

June found a copy of *Valley of the Dolls* upstairs in Annette's room, and I decided that was how she'd come by her injuries—Annette had figured out who had taken it, but stubborn June had refused to confess. The spine was worn at the dirtiest parts before we ever got our hands on it; all we had to do was let it fall open. We especially liked a scene that took place in a swimming pool.

"Listen," June would say. In a high voice, she said, " 'Oh Ted, not in the water, don't,' " then, gruffly, " 'Why not. We've done it every other way.' "

It was that line that grabbed at my stomach. Every other way. I couldn't imagine many other ways—truth be told, if it hadn't been for *Valley of the Dolls*, I wouldn't have been able to imagine one. I knew the physical details, but I had no notion that most people did such things lying down. That information was not part of my mother's informative talks: and then the man puts this here, as if he were replacing a quart of milk in an empty fridge.

One day, after June had read that scene out loud three times, she said: "We could do that."

"We don't have a swimming pool," I said cautiously.

"No duh," she said. "Come here."

I followed her to the bedroom she shared with her mother, who was upstairs visiting her parents. Through the small window, the sunset looked like June's black eye. I could see my father smoking on the porch, scanning the street. June flicked on the overhead light. The dresser drawers were missing half their pulls; Terry's bed was a jumble of sheets and huge nylon underpants. June's cot had been folded up and tucked in a corner.

She crawled into her mother's bed. "Okay. I'm the girl and you're the man."

"I don't want to be the man," I said. In the games of play that I knew, the best parts were always female.

She stretched out on her back. "Get on me."

"Sit on you?"

"Sit here," she said, and touched the front pockets of her shorts. I climbed onto her and rested, side-saddle; she took one of my ankles and spun me so that I was straddling her.

"Now," she said. "Pretend you're madly in love with me."

"How?"

She bucked me with her hips. I was so small I nearly bounced off her, but I felt too big. Big enough to hurt her just with my weight, too close to the ceiling, getting bigger all the time. I hated it, I said, "I don't want to play."

"We're having sex," said June.

"We are *not*. I'm not that dumb."

"Okay, we're pretending. Go on."

"I don't know how," I told her.

"Yes you do."

I looked at her stupidly, empty of questions.

She sighed, the way she did when she explained anything—cowlicks, kickball—that escaped me.

"Okay. Get off and lie down."

I did, and she climbed on me.

"You're so pretty," she said. For a minute I thought maybe she meant it—she said it in her usual angry tone—but I saw her dreamy face and understood she was pretending.

"Turn off the light," I whispered.

She said, "I want to see you." That was a line from *Valley of the Dolls,* and I knew she said it to win me over. But her eyes were closed, the good one and the black one, which was turning into stripes of color. I managed to reach over to snap off the lamp, which only made the light from the living room brighter.

"Shut the door," I said.

"Nobody's here." She spread her hands on the air and moved them awhile. I thought she was casting a spell. Then she said, "You have great big boobies."

I laughed out loud. She tried to open her black eye, but couldn't raise the lid fully or angrily enough, so she closed it and rearranged her hips, still sitting up. Suddenly she lay down on top of me, our hips aligned, legs touching the length, though my toes were up against her shins. She stuck her face in mine—and sometimes, still, when I kiss a man, it's June's face I see, and it seems a pity that everyone looks so similar close up, but now it's obvious I'm stalling, because it's not true. She was a little girl with a crusty lip and a bruised face, her eyes tight, which I thought must have hurt. She swished her hips a little.

"June," I said, my stomach jumping. All the time I'd been in Boston, I felt dumb, because there were so many things I didn't know. Before, I was cocky and assumed I'd always owned my knowledge: I remembered the lessons but not the teacher. Suddenly, I realized, some things you must be taught.

"How do you know this?" I asked.

"You know," she said.

"I don't. Tell me."

"Brian," she whispered in my ear. "He'll show you, too, if you want. He told me not to tell anybody else, but I bet he would."

I was quiet and horrified. Annette's greasy boyfriend. I hadn't ever heard him say anything; I'd thought of him as harmless, maybe the only harmless person in the whole house.

June opened her eyes, the good one as narrow as the bad. "I think," she said, "I think we should take our clothes off."

I'd never heard June say anything tentatively. It made me brave.

"I want to go home," I said.

She still had me pinned. "Phoebe," she said. It was not the Man talking to the Girl; it was just June, lonely in the dark. I reached up and touched her hair and felt another scratch beneath. I whispered, "I don't want to do this."

She rolled off me and snorted. "Shoulda known," she said, back to old June. Then she sat up and combed her hair with her fingers. She was wearing a red tank top, and when she let her arm drop, one strap slid down her shoulder.

"What's your father looking for?" she asked, nodding toward the window.

I got up and started for the bedroom door. "I don't know. Whoever's doing the stuff to the cars and houses."

"Well," she said, hitching up her top, looking at me for just a second, "he'll never catch me."

I tried to get her eye again without saying anything, but couldn't. When I said, "June," she did look up at me, and stared, and rubbed her shoulder, and we both understood that this was a threat. Nothing more could be said.

When I went out the front door, Brian and Annette were drinking on the porch. I stood in the doorway, hating them.

"Hey Feeble," said Annette. "Shithead. Having fun?"

I was going so fast my foot didn't even touch her outstretched leg.

In bed that night, I touched my hips where June's hips had been. I didn't want to think about that afternoon, because every time I did, I wondered if Brian and Annette had been peering through the window, watching us. Sometimes I thought: maybe they didn't see. Sometimes I thought: thank God I didn't take off my clothes. I did not think of June and what she had said about my father not catching her: thinking about it risked telling; telling meant terrible danger for me, I was sure.

In the morning we heard that three of the neighborhood cats had been killed, each one strangled with twine.

* * *

My father's vigilance was not paying off; my mother thought his worry was silly. Still, Dad took to sleeping on the sofa, hoping to hear footsteps in the night. A ridiculous hope, since he slept heavily, noisy himself. When I went out that night in my pajamas, he didn't even move.

I had never been outside by myself so late. I could hear a car whooshing down the busy street at the end of the block and then just some faint clicking, streetlights or electrical lines. Even Mac's was closed now, I knew—and they were only closed four hours of every day, 1 A.M. to 5. Nobody's lights were on. The street, at least, was asleep.

I took a crowbar from the Friels' parking lot, crept partway down the street, and started swinging. Puny me, I couldn't lift the bar to reach the newly repaired windshields, rearview mirrors: I went right for the bodies of the cars, and the bar was heavy enough to leave deep dents, the paint flecked off in the middle. My arms got tired after a few cars, and I left the crowbar in the gutter.

Did June feel like this? I threw a handful of rocks at a car; they clattered to the ground without effect. The truth was I didn't know exactly what I felt. June has been keeping secrets, I know I thought that much. At the same time, I was furious at her for letting me know, for giving me a secret, too. I pushed at a rearview mirror with my bare hands, punched at it with the heel of my palm. Not a thing. June was better at this than I was, better even at this. I kicked a chain-link fence and listened to it shiver.

As I leaned on the fence, trying to pull it out of shape, I wondered what would make a person do something like this. There I was doing it, and I still didn't understand. Maybe if I'd done it more than one night, I would have figured it out, but I was caught, of course, not only by my father but several neighbors and one policeman who, since the cat murders, had decided it was time to patrol the neighborhood.

I was sent to a battery of psychologists, who thought they understood why I'd admit to everything but the cats. It wasn't fear for myself or disgust, but a simple love of cats. I didn't want my parents to forbid me from ever having one.

I was grounded, of course: less for punishment, more because my parents believed I needed constant love, reprimands, snacks. My mother watched me with sad eyes, sure she was the one who'd caused me to do such despicable things; she thought it was her ambivalence about the new neighborhood that made me so angry at it.

"Invite your friends over," she said. "Ask June to come in."

But I'd lost June. She would not talk to me or let me come near. Sometimes I'd see her at the end of the street. I'd recognize her right away: no one else stood like June, with her feet wide apart and her hands resting in her back pockets. When I went to look for her, she was gone.

I took to visiting Terry, June's mother. She was the only one who treated me as she had before; maybe she expected all kids to go bad eventually. I sat on the porch with her while she drank, and she told me the neighborhood gossip. The old woman who lived across the street made her husband sleep on the porch; the fat girl next door was pregnant. I thought I'd earned it, that I now belonged to the neighborhood and maybe even to this family, and June would come to recognize that. We'd be sisters, the way she'd suggested we might be if my mother left Watertown.

Finally Terry told me that I shouldn't hang around so much,

because June wouldn't come home if I were anywhere near the house.

"She'd stay out all night," said Terry. "Probably like it fine. But you know, she's my kid and you got parents and you got a house."

I wish I could say that things worked out for June, that I had somehow saved her. But I took blame I was unworthy of and therefore got attention that was likewise not mine: so many people asking me what was wrong, what had moved me, that eventually I felt loved and interesting. This was all rightly June's. I wasn't sixteen till I realized she might have needed it; it was some time after that I realized she might not have gotten it anyhow, not the way I did, because of who she was and who I was. Because of who our parents were.

The next year, she went to the local junior high and I was sent to one across town—"A change of venue," my father called it—and when we saw each other, we said nothing, hurried into our houses.

Sometimes I dreamed of moving again, so I could relive the scene I still remembered clearly from Portland: one little girl in the back window of a car, another on the pavement, both crying and making promises. I was sure if I left Watertown June and I could be friends again. But we both continued to grow up on that street, and I went to college and June got pregnant and married. All the old businesses are gone now, the buildings torn down and replaced by Italian restaurants. But when I visit my parents, I still see June, her two children, though her husband is nowhere in evidence. It might be her I see, sitting on the porch in the black night, sipping at the air through a cigarette.

SECRETARY OF STATE

I

BENNY, FANNIE, ROSEY, MOSEY, Abie, Libby, Idy, Sadie, Essie: the Barron brood in descending order of age, my mother, the baby, at the tail end. She could recite the names faster than anybody, until they blurred into a poem, a nursery rhyme, a run of music—Benny to Essie in two seconds flat. It didn't matter that Uncle Abraham had always been called Bram, never Abie; it didn't matter that Uncle Mose couldn't stand that sweet *y* at the end of his name. She'd race through to hit all of them, each a base that had to be touched. You'd think she was afraid if she forgot to say one name aloud, that brother or sister might disappear or, worse and more likely, find out and take it badly. A sudden knock at the kitchen window, a stern familiar face pressed against the glass.

They could do anything, these people.

It wasn't that my mother married an inventor that bothered them; it was that she didn't marry Thomas Alva Edison himself. Of course, had Edison come calling for little Essie, her brothers and sisters would have found plenty wrong with him, too.

True enough, like most inventors, my father was not quite successful. Not a failure in the usual sense, because what he invented frequently worked. My childhood was full of small comforts of his devising: self-turning magazine stands, a never-fail ice cream scoop, furniture that folded up neat as books. Big things, too. As a young man working for Eli Lilly, he invented an anesthetic for heart patients that is still used today, but because he was a salaried chemist, he got neither money nor credit for it. This was seen as a great tragedy among my mother's family, who thought credit was vital to living. Only my Uncle Ellis—a non-Barron—admired Dad for the pure wonder of the invention. "Whenever I see your father," Ellis once told me, "I think: this man has saved more lives than anyone I know."

Despite my father's life-saving tendencies, my mother, under the direction of her family, convinced him to quit his chemist's job. The Barrons, the Aunts and Uncles, voted on everything. What course of action should the U.S. take abroad? What movies deserved to be popular? Were Sacco and Vanzetti guilty? Unlike Lyndon Johnson and John Wayne, my father had the good sense to have married into the Barron family, and was therefore obliged to follow their counsel. There are times I thought—still do—that I had ten parents who fell into two camps: my father, and the Barrons. My practical education I got entirely from Dad: how to cook, order airplane tickets by telephone, how to install venetian blinds and rewire a lamp and drive and iron and balance a meal. He taught me the alphabet, algebra, thrift. My mother, on the other hand, filled me with Barron philosophy. Be brave, be recklessly truthful, be smart and funny and entertaining. But the Barrons couldn't tell me how to do these things, and the skills I inherited from my father were the skills of a modest man.

Most of the Aunts and Uncles lived near Chicago, near us, where they'd grown up. Only a couple of them scattered—my uncle Bram was a doctor in Indianapolis; Ben lived in St. Louis; Aunt Libby had married a crazy dentist and moved with him to Vermont. In the minds of the Aunts and Uncles, you'd have to be crazy to live in Vermont. Every now and then, one of them would storm off there for a visit and return with stories of the odd, taciturn inhabitants; primitive and inedible meals; all that green, as if Vermont had been left unattended and had gone bad. "Move all those mountains and trees," you could hear them tell the natives, "and then we'll teach you how to make the perfect soft-boiled egg. You'll be up to snuff in no time."

None of my mother's brothers and sisters had large families—only one or two children, though Libby in Vermont had three. No mystery there—though they liked the company of their siblings, I think they each felt short-changed somehow. I imagine each Barron in bed soon after his or her wedding: the new spouse says, "Lots of kids, don't you think? Let's have a bunch," and the Barron, without so much as a romantic pause, says, "Honey, I'm the expert on that. Let's not."

Instead, they stuck with the original big family. They got together every Sunday for what was basically an organized brawl with refreshments. The Aunts and Uncles dressed up in their best, although they were not snappy dressers. They appreciated nice clothes and good bargains, but there was usually something slightly off in the execution—I don't think my mother ever wore anything that wasn't a little snug across the bust; skinny Aunt Sadie favored stiff dark skirts that made her look like an umbrella blown wrong by the wind. Uncle Mose's patterned shirts never quite gave up the squares they'd been folded into in the drawer: he was as relaxed and garish and dizzying as a well-read map.

My mother was closest to Ida of all her siblings. Aunt Ida was exactly like Mom, but more so. She was heavier, but in the same bosomy, skinny-legged way; her voice cracked constantly in the broad nasal twang that my mother's only tended toward. She was even more of a worrier and had to say aloud every small fear that crossed my mother's mind.

My mother had been Ida's responsibility when they were children: every older Barron had a younger Barron to take care of. Ida, a fretter even as a child, would once a month get up in the middle of the night and dress my mother before leading her out to the lawn. It wasn't that she'd smelled smoke, exactly: it was just that she'd remembered a fire was possible.

Fire was possible, death was possible, a broken nose because of a careless shoelace was downright inevitable. Ida wasn't a pessimist. Worry was her religion, *what if* the mantra that kept disaster away. *What if* and *I knew someone once* and *I just know it*. And my mother was Ida's disciple. On the cold grass those nights as a child, she'd learned. Fire was possible, but there was never a fire. They must be doing something right.

The Sunday that my father decided he'd had enough of the Barrons was like any other. Aunt Ida met us at the door.

"Sophie, honey," she said to me, "do you want some ice cream?" Aunt Ida's freezer was always burdened with ice cream, and she was burdened with the duty of giving it away.

"No thank you," I said, because my mother was there and I was supposed to be losing weight. My mother's idea of a diet was to make me turn down any food not offered directly by her. This meant I ate only twice as much as most people.

"Sure you want ice cream," said Aunt Ida.

"Honest, no."

Aunt Ida stared at my father, as if she were trying to place him. Finally, she said, "Come on in, Frank." We stepped into the living room.

"She didn't care," Aunt Rose was saying. "She just sent that poor woman right out of the house, with a child and everything."

"She was hard," said Uncle Mose.

"That's just how she was," said my mother, taking off her coat.

"How who was?" I asked.

"Abraham's wife," said my mother. "Sarah. From Genesis."

My father was still by the door. He usually spent these sessions in the kitchen, with Uncle Ellis, Ida's husband. He looked like he couldn't decide on the safest path through the Barrons. I was about to go to him—I felt somewhat at peril myself—when Aunt Ida tapped me on the shoulder.

"Would you like some ice cream," she asked.

"No thank you," I said.

My father steered me to the kitchen, or I steered him. Uncle Ellis sat at the table, reading a newspaper and fingering a deck of cards. Having been driven to his kitchen, he refused to be forced out the door entirely.

"Howdyadoodle," he said to me. My father sat down across from him.

"I have some neopolitan, and some sherbet," Aunt Ida said, leaning over the breakfast bar into the kitchen.

"Sophie doesn't want any ice cream," my mother called in from the living room.

"Let her decide for herself," said Aunt Ida. "You think that's good for her, just to be led along? What happens when she gets married." She looked at me, her face grave, as if this were the truest test of my character. "Which one?"

"Neither," I told her.

"See?" said my mother.

"What else could she say? She's polite, she doesn't want to get her mother mad. Later, maybe."

I heard Aunt Sadie say from the living room, "Rose, you've said some pretty crazy things in your life, but that's about the craziest."

"Oh for Pete's *sake,"* said Rose.

"What?" said Aunt Ida.

"Rose," said Aunt Sadie, "thinks that Manet is a better painter than Monet."

"Monet," said Aunt Rose, "is pure fluff."

Uncle Ellis shook his head. "Marriage," he said to me, and laughed. "Your aunt Ida wants to know about you getting married? Look at me." He started shuffling the cards. "Here I think I'm marrying one woman, and it turns out I'm marrying half a dozen."

"Ellis," said Aunt Ida.

"You didn't marry me," shouted Aunt Sadie, who never married. "If you asked, I would have said no."

"Half a dozen very nice women," said Uncle Ellis. "And a girl as pretty as you, Sadie? A man as handsome as me? Don't be so sure what you would have said."

"Talk sense," said Aunt Ida. She put down something cold at my elbow.

"What's this?" I asked.

She had a look of innocence on her face. "It's the ice cream you asked for."

Uncle Ellis started dealing the cards. "Just another Sunday," he said. After he dealt one card he reached out and, with the tips of his fingers, patted my father's knuckles. "Don't worry, Frank," he said. "A couple more hours, that's all."

The Barrons themselves did not play cards. They saw gin as simply a distraction to conversation. I sat in the kitchen with Ellis and Dad, happy to listen to the usual Barron *mishegoss* filtering across the breakfast bar. Somehow, I loved my mother best when she was with her family: she was funny and quick in a way she never was at home; she got mad in a way that thrilled me; she turned beautiful, all her coloring darker and dramatic. Sometimes she took me into her lap and combed my hair absent-mindedly. She never got nervous at all. On the way home from Ida's, I would miss that version of my mother, knowing I would not meet her for another week. It was like a bright light went through my mother when she was at her best, and it lit up all the other holes in her character.

I heard Aunt Ida say, "We're very worried about Tillie."

Usually, Aunt Ida and Mom played this game alone when Ida and my cousin Tillie came to visit us. Ida and Mom would pick a worry and describe together what could go wrong. First they'd be serious, but soon as the worries got worse, they'd take a certain odd turn. Bad posture? Tillie marries a hunchback. Reckless eating habits? I run away and join the circus as a combination fat lady, sword swallower, and circus geek, "the girl who'll swallow anything," my slogan. Tillie is hit by a car, lives, but has CADILLAC backward forever emblazoned on her forehead. I never get married and eventually open a museum of dirt; I stand on the sidewalk and call people in.

It was our mothers' way of warding off bad luck, their own peculiar way to tell the evil eye: these are unappetizing children, nothing for you here. They'd learned it from their father, who, when registering his children at school, would not say exactly how many there were; to count was bad luck, and you couldn't tell who or what would overhear the total, and figure there were extra. "A lot," he'd say. "Let's just say enough."

Today's future had to do with Tillie's fear of the boys at school: she thought they were rough and ugly. Soon that moved on to a general discussion of Tillie's romantic future. Aunt Ida worried that Tillie would marry the first man who treated her with kindness. I went into the living room: I loved to hear Tillie's ruinations. She was four years younger than me, girlish and stingy with her things and extremely pretty.

Aunt Ida said, "Tillie will fall in love with an organ grinder. The kind with a monkey."

"Italian," said my mother.

"Italian," said Aunt Sadie, "and old."

Uncle Mose sat up in his chair. "So's the monkey. Very old. An aged monkey."

"But he loves Tillie—"

"The organ grinder loves her," said my mother.

"Yes, the organ grinder," agreed Aunt Ida. "The monkey can take or leave her. Actually, no—the monkey hates her. The monkey is prone to biting."

"Worse and worse," said my mother. "And the organ grinder isn't very good at his job."

Aunt Ida regarded my mother. "How can you be bad at organ grinding?"

"His heart isn't in it. He isn't jolly. It was his father's business."

"A tragic organ grinder," said Uncle Mose. "Of course."

"So," said my mother. "They're in love, so they get married. But business is off."

Tillie stood up suddenly. "Stop," she said.

"And then," said Aunt Ida.

"I won't," said Tillie. She climbed into her mother's lap. "I'm not," she said. Poor Tillie. It did seem to me that while I was seen as somebody who'd destroy herself through shoddy habits and worse taste, Tillie merely drifted into bad luck, accepting miserable marriage proposals, dropping herself into the hands of unfriendly mobs.

"Please," she said to my mother and Aunt Ida, as if she thought they wanted to make her do these things. But they couldn't stop—if they ended before the worst came, if they left the story when it was merely bad, not impossible, it broke the spell. Tillie had to hear herself taken to the edge of disaster and over, just as she had a million times before. Fire was possible, and there was only one way to keep it from occurring.

Tillie curled up in her mother's lap, trying to look like she needed protection, but Aunt Ida could only stroke her hair and offer ice cream, all the time saying, "And then the organ grinder's monkey dies, tragic, and they are so poor, and Tillie is so thin, she has to wear the monkey's hand-me-downs. Finally she is buried in a little bell-boy's costume, her very best outfit."

"Maammaa," Tillie wailed.

"A nice outfit," said Aunt Ida. "The monkey only wore it once."

My father hated to hear these prophesies as much as Tillie did. I saw him walk to the doorway, frowning. My father was movie-star handsome—that's what the Barrons said, though they made it sound like a flaw. Now his dark hair was raked down on one side, his blue eyes serious. Bad enough that Ida and Esther talked about such things at home, just the two of them. But here with everybody. He waved at my mother to get her attention and said, "Esther."

My mother waved back, but Aunt Sadie was talking to her, and she took my mother by the wrist to reclaim her attention.

"Girls are sensitive," said Aunt Ida, Tillie curled up in her lap.

"Some, yes," said Aunt Rose.

"Well," said my father. He cleared his throat. "Can you blame her?"

"Well," said Aunt Rose, "that's just the sort of attitude I think spoils children."

Aunt Sadie, from across the room, said, "Frequently men are awkward with little girls."

"Not all men," said Uncle Mose.

"No, not all men, but some. If you haven't been brought up around girls, sometimes you don't know how to treat them."

They turned away from my father and began to argue about

what could possibly make a man behave as he just had, never mentioning him again.

I suppose the unhappy prophesies could have frightened me as much as they did Tillie and my father. Part of it was just that—if they bothered Tillie, who I disliked, I wanted to savor them. I could not believe they were really about me, any more than I believed in the card tricks my father sometimes showed me. They were the Barron brand of magic. They were about some poor fatherless girl who happened to have my name and face and all my bad habits. A dirt curator? I'd start in my head to see this museum, the steady heaps of Georgia red clay, of city *shmutz,* of lint, mud, tar, crumbs. I'd tend them lovingly.

I believed my father would save me from any bad future. I think this might have been one of the reasons my mother played the game: she saw that I was beginning to favor my father, and sending me over Niagara Falls in a barrel was the only way she knew to take me from him. At the moment just before catastrophe, she was my best hope in the world.

On the way home in the car, my father said, "Do you have to do that?"

"What?" my mother asked.

"Those terrible futures," Dad said. "I can barely stand listening to them. They're morbid. I don't see how you can bring yourself to say some of those things."

My mother turned to look at him. "I have to make myself."

We turned the corner onto our street. "Why on earth do it?"

My mother set her hands on her lap and stared at them. "Ida and I love our daughters," she said. "To imagine the worst things that could happen to them . . . well, that's the worst thing that could happen to us. If we can manage to say every bad thing, we can manage to get through anything." She turned to me, in the back seat. "It breaks my heart to say those things, you know."

My father pulled into the driveway and shut off the car. "Esther, Esther," he said, looking out the windshield. "Why do you have to break your own heart?"

In the house, we drifted off to our usual places. Dad went to the kitchen, I headed for the basement, my mother retreated to her den. While I read on the floor of the rec room, my father appeared suddenly on the stairs. He walked down, deep in thought.

"Perhaps I should do the laundry," he said, picking up a bottle of detergent from a basket of dirty clothing. He had a way of making every idea seem as if it had just then occurred to him. "Soap, starch, bleach. You shouldn't mix bleach and ammonia, Sophie. The fumes are fatal." He started the laundry. Then he wandered through the basement, looking for loose socks, perhaps, one more little chore to do. The washing machine sloshed and choked. Every now and then, Dad would stop and tap my bottom affectionately with the toe of his shoe.

He walked to the far end of the room and peered out through one of the little windows near the ceiling, though all he could see was the length of aluminum fence that kept the dirt back, some rocks, the edge of the lawn.

"Your mother," he said, "should learn how to drive."

"Why?" I asked. Mom had never known. It was one of the many things my father took care of; he treated my mother with the sort of deference one awards to great thinkers.

"Well." He played with the little curtain in the window, then let it fall. "I think she should take the two of you to the Barrons' from now on. I mean, they don't want me there."

"Yes they do." I sat up and closed my book. But I knew it wasn't so; I had heard my mother and her siblings talk about their spouses before, as if the rest of the world were part of some other family, a badly raised one. "Well, he's not as bright as us," they'd say about a husband—I'd heard it about my father. I'm ashamed to say that something in me might have even believed them, they were so sure of themselves.

"No," he said. And he turned back and winked. The washing machine kicked into a new cycle. "And guess what? I don't want to be there myself. They won't worry me anymore. So. You think she'll go for it?"

I lay back on my stomach, reopened my book. I wanted to seem casual. "Does this mean I can stay home, too?"

My father laughed and walked toward me. "You," he said, "are part of that family. You belong there, Sophie, and if I kept you with me I'd never be forgiven. Not by anybody." He tapped me with his foot; I looked up and smiled. Then he caressed the small of my back with his outstretched toe.

My father loved the pure physical fact of me and did sneaky things to get near. When I did homework at the dining room table, he'd stand behind my chair and lean over. In the kitchen, he'd reach around me elaborately to get a cooking utensil; he'd give me a taste from a spoon, holding my chin to steady. My collars always needed his straightening; my face wanted cleaning with a soft handkerchief he'd spit into. It was as if he realized there was something he desperately craved but could not bear to ask for, and decided to make that thing so unalterably part of his daily job nobody could deny him. He'd bawl me out for messiness, but his voice stayed careful, happy. I let him be the expert: I let myself get sloppier and sloppier, ready for my father's calm hand to prepare me for the world.

I was, in fact, allowed to come along on most of the driving lessons, and thought that I understood the whole business better than my mother did. She got impatient when my father occasionally turned around and explained things to me—how a spark plug fired, for instance, something my mother felt had nothing whatsoever to do with the business at hand.

For the final lesson, she drove us all the way to Aunt Ida's one Sunday afternoon. Mom drove the way she did everything. She threw her whole body into it and delivered a running commentary on what was happening. Her foot jammed the clutch; she'd make sudden furtive grabs for the stick shift, as if she didn't want it to see her sneaking up.

"Oh you," she said to an understandably wary milk truck. "What are you doing? Come on, guy, just go around me." We were at a stoplight, on a hill, and my mother, who wasn't good at hill starts, refused to go with someone right behind her.

"It's okay, Esther," my father said. "You know how to do this. Just relax."

"He's scared of you," I said from the back seat.

"Me? I'm scared of him. I'm just a little person. Look at the size of that driver." My mother believed that with her at the wheel, our large green Chevy became somehow like her: a well-intentioned car, slightly nervous, with beautiful manners. She stuck her hand out the window and waved him around. This was my mother's main talent—waiting things out.

When we got to Aunt Ida's, my mother strolled up the walk

waving the car keys, as if they were a lovely piece of jewelry my father had finally given her.

"Are you coming in, Frank," Aunt Ida asked from the porch.

I looked at my father, who leaned up against the fender of the car, watching my mother flash the keys; I was just two steps behind her. Dad smiled at nobody in particular. Before he could answer, Aunt Ida turned to Mom and said, "Don't tell me you drove here."

Mom nodded; I could hear Aunt Sadie, inside, say, instead of hello, "Driving? Driving's easy, once you know how." She didn't know how to drive herself, but it was clear she could have if she'd wanted to.

"Maybe," said my father, quietly. He pulled himself onto the hood of the car, and looked foolish and happy. "Maybe I'll come in, and maybe I won't."

My father kept good on his promise not to let the Barrons get to him for a while. Or at least he seemed to. He still saw them in small doses or at holidays, and I always thought he seemed more at ease than he had been. Sometimes he made nasty jokes; once, at a diner, he willfully levitated the table and spilled Aunt Ida's iced tea and wouldn't stop laughing. Other times around them, he stayed deep in his thoughts, removed himself as much as he could. And though I kept going to Aunt Ida's, where they never missed Dad at all, I thought the Barrons in this way lost most of their power over me: I grew up my father's girl.

II

UNCLE BENNY WAS THE FAMILY DANDY, THE OLDEST BROTHER. When he visited from Missouri, he always came fresh from the dry cleaner's. He smelled that way, too, like delicious scorched steam. He was older than my parents by ten years, and a hot-shot, a show-off. These were the Barron words for him, said with a combination of admiration and bewilderment. Ben was in real estate, which the Barrons did not quite approve of or understand.

We couldn't tell whether or not Ben was successful. He lived in St. Louis, with Aunt Lillian, a pale woman entirely eclipsed by her husband. They only came to town every now and then. Ben didn't settle into chatting; he paced through the house, patting the thick folder of papers in his inside pocket: train tickets, business notes, phone numbers, his own business cards, which he handed to children as if they were an educational toy.

We, on the other hand, were not successful, and struggled for money more than the rest of the family. My father, after he quit the job at Lilly's, never quite settled down with another. He taught for a while, then wrote textbooks and a science column for a national scholastic magazine, things that would let him tinker around the house. Later, he was part-owner in a restaurant.

After his restaurant failed, Dad told me, "I find it so sad that there aren't enough meals in life for all the menus I've assembled." A pot of creamy soup was bubbling on the stove; a pan of cornbread browned in the oven. You never knew what you might hit when you bit into my father's cornbread. Dad, the chemist, was always looking for a miraculous assemblage.

"I'm going to help you out," Uncle Benny said to my father one night soon after the restaurant went under.

"Don't do me any favors, Ben," said Dad.

"No, really. I got an idea, need a partner."

"I'm no businessman," said my father. "You need somebody who is."

"No," said Uncle Benny. "Look, it's this way. Esther is my sister, and I naturally want things to be as good for her as they can be. Let me be honest, I don't need a partner for this, but it's a good deal, you'll make some money, you won't have long to wait . . ."

"Ben," says my father.

"Really, Frank. Trust me," says Uncle Benny.

Or something. I was not there when my father agreed to be Uncle Ben's business partner in an apartment deal in St. Louis. I don't know what Uncle Ben said to convince Dad that the apartments were a sound proposition; I had heard my father say to my mother that he never wanted to go into business again in his life. But why should he doubt Ben? In his perfect hat, razor-sharp clothing, Ben looked like he knew what he was talking about. No doubt he said as much: "Frank, you're not a businessman. Take some advice from one who knows. Take the deal."

Mom took the case up with the Barrons, who were unanimous: of course, invest with Ben. Ben was brilliant, a business genius. Dad would be crazy not to do this.

And the fact of the matter is it was the first time the Barrons invited my father into anything. That must have meant the world to him; he must have thought that at least this part of his life was taking a turn for the better.

So my father invested, and the Barrons were thrilled. It made Dad uneasy, everyone knowing his business, but they all congratulated him. "Ben knows," Uncle Mose said significantly. "You're taken care of."

Soon my father got excited about it. Anything that was a chance for research delighted him, and he checked out a dozen books on real estate from the library. His life seemed aimless to him after he quit his job at the pharmaceutical place, and he latched on to interests with the hope they'd turn into passions. In fact, my father got so caught up in the whole thing that he decided to go to a Sunday meeting with us for the first time since my mother had learned to drive. Maybe he felt like he was part of the family, and wanted to celebrate. I had graduated from high school and enrolled at the University of Chicago on a scholarship; I had a job and a little apartment in town. But I came back almost every weekend, missing my parents even though they were just thirty minutes away.

The Aunts and Uncles were on their favorite daydream: who would do what when the Barrons took over the government. The argument always ended the same way: Ida, of course, would head the Library of Congress; Dr. Uncle Bram would be Surgeon General. Uncle Benny, Aunt Fannie, and Uncle Mose all had their law degrees, and so there was some argument about who would be Attorney General. It was generally agreed that they'd be on the Supreme Court, and then that sounded so good that they all wanted to be Supreme Court justices, and that started a new argument: who was too hot-headed to judge, too emotional, too sleepy. The Barron Court. They would have loved that, to listen carefully to the evidence of somebody's life and then adjourn together to convince one another of what was right.

My father looked around the room. He put a hand on my shoulder and said, "Stay close."

Aunt Rose said, "Mose should be President." You could tell by her tone of voice that she wanted somebody to say, "No, you, Rose. You'd be terrific."

Instead, Sadie said, "A President needs a First Lady."

"Buchanan," said Aunt Ida in her best librarian voice, "was not married."

"Ben should be President," said Aunt Sadie, "because he's married, looks good, is smart."

"Lillian as First Lady?" my mother asked incredulously.

"Oh, I'd get divorced after the election," said Ben. Aunt Lillian had stayed behind in St. Louis, and he felt no loyalty toward her.

"Ben would get the votes," said Sadie. "He's a wheeler-dealer. Objectively speaking, I think he'd get elected."

"I am not a wheeler-dealer," said Uncle Ben. "I am a businessman."

"I meant," said Aunt Sadie, "you're very *political*."

The Barrons agreed on Benjamin Barron as the Barron candidate for President.

"And I'm head of the Library of Congress," said Aunt Ida, sure of her position.

They handed out posts carefully, a little grudgingly. I was allowed Ambassador to Spain, because I was getting my degree in Spanish. "It's Mexico or Spain," said my mother, "and Mexico is close." That was an argument for Mexico—surely, if I were Ambassador to Mexico, I would get home more often—but I was awarded Spain because the Aunts and Uncles agreed that it was a nicer country.

"I'd like to be Secretary of State," said my father, all of a sudden.

Uncle Mose cleared his throat; Aunt Sadie scratched something out of her dark skirt. You had to be nominated for a post among the Barrons, you couldn't just claim one.

"Why?" said Ida.

"Sounds like a good job," said Dad. "Sounds like fun."

"But what are your qualifications?" asked Ida.

Dad shrugged. "I'm level-headed."

Aunt Ida shook her head. "Look, you're the nervous type; you aren't aggressive enough." Then she caught herself—she was the hostess, after all—and turned kindly. "I mean, I don't think you'd like the job."

Dad said, and I couldn't tell how seriously, "Please?"

"No," said Aunt Ida. "I'm sorry, but no."

Mom patted Dad's shoulder. "You'll live in the embassy, with Sophie," she said. "You'll hardly miss it."

"Honestly," I said. "Do we have to talk like this? Can't we just have a normal conversation?"

"This is normal," said Mose.

"Of course it is," said Rose.

"Sophie," said my mother, "isn't this a normal conversation?"

I sighed. A college lady, I felt newly weary around my family. "Under the circumstances, sure."

"Under what circumstances," asked Aunt Ida.

"Under the Barron rules of order."

"But your friends at school," said Uncle Mose, "your friends don't talk like this."

"No."

Uncle Mose poured himself a cup of coffee. "Not talkative people, your friends?"

"Well, yes," I said. "But they don't try so hard to be . . . controversial. They just talk about personal stuff, just chat."

The Aunts and Uncles looked serious for a minute. Uncle Mose lit a cigarette and, with the match still lit, brushed his hair back. Then he blew out some smoke.

He said, "Sometimes I sleep in pajamas and sometimes I don't."

The Aunts and Uncles launched their arguments with this conceit, all at the same time.

Ben called within a month after he'd first brought up the proposition, summertime. Not contrite; he just explained that he'd guessed wrong. The apartments were in bad shape, and after they'd spent the invested money on fixing up the place, the floors had collapsed. Too bad; they would have done well for themselves, but, well, said Uncle Benny—business is business. Next time he had something, he promised, he'd call.

When my father hung up, he looked tired. His eyes got wet; he apologized for no reason. A little later in the day, a few tears dropped. He said, "I am not available for dinner."

I stayed downstairs while my mother went to tend to my father.

"Call me if you need me," I said.

"You bet."

She did not call me; she did not come back down.

I sat on the sofa for a long time. I raised my hands and imagined putting them on my father's shoulders to comfort him, but couldn't call up what I would say. This was all selfishness, I thought, to be worried about my inabilities when I should be worried about what was happening, and that made me feel worse: I was useless and selfish; I could not do anything for my father.

My worry pushed me up the stairs. I paused outside my parents' door and heard them talking. A good sign, I thought; I'd been raised to think that dialogue was the road to everything. When I leaned closer, I heard my father, sobbing, saying over and over, "Essie, Essie, you have to help me. You have to help me." Beneath this, my mother repeated her own chorus: "I don't know what to do. I just do not know."

"I'm driving," my mother said.

I shook my head. "I'll do it."

"No," she said. So I got into the back seat with my father, who was almost asleep. I did not know what had happened to him, but my mother, calm, in charge, said that we should take him to the hospital immediately. She drove more smoothly than she ever had in her life, as if to say to my father, You taught me this.

Dad's dead weight scared me. He smelled of bitter mint. I wanted to talk to him, but I could only lean on the back of the front seat, saying to my mother, "Left here. Keep going. Get in the left lane. Turn." We both knew that if I stopped talking to her, or if she stopped listening to me, we would not be able to go on.

I helped my mother fill out the forms, and thereby learned everything about my father I did not know. His age, for instance, which he had for some reason doctored. I didn't know that this was his third breakdown—he'd had one in graduate school, and then another while he worked for Eli Lilly, before I was born. I did not know that my father was the sort of man who, in sorrow, would eat the contents of the medicine cabinet, including diet pills, three sleeping tablets, No Doz, aspirin, cough syrup, and an entire tube of toothpaste.

My mother knew and never told me.

Because I had not been home, I didn't realize how bad my father had been, that my mother had to grocery shop in small trips three times a week because my father had developed a habit of cooking everything in the house. He'd been depressed for some time, my mother told me, and I thought I should have noticed. After my father's nervous breakdown, I saw his sadness beforehand everywhere: in the way he always had to have a pot of something on the stove; in his clothing, which was always caked with his foods; in the way he treated any restaurant we went to, his tenderness with the silver.

Even in the way, three months before, he had so gently asked for the post of Secretary of State. If my father had felt well, he would have announced that the day the Barrons took over the government was the day he defected to Canada.

"I'm to blame," my mother said.

"Of course not," I told her. We sat in the molded hospital chairs. "You didn't know."

"No," she said. "I'm the one who made him lie in the first place. I asked him to."

"Why on earth?" I asked.

"What would the family have said? Seven years younger than me? Already a nervous breakdown? They never would have accepted him. Your father knows science. My family—that's my only real expertise. I would have lost them."

"Who cares?" I said, now angry at everybody involved.

"Me," she said. She held her own hand, as if it belonged to a frightened stranger she wanted to calm. "I loved your father too much to not marry him—" she shook her head, "—but I loved my family too much to disappoint them. I mean, imagine Ida knowing. It would have kept her up nights for decades."

He was born in Queens, not Connecticut. He'd had cancer as a child and was not expected to live. His mother's maiden name was Reilly. He'd been prone to depression all his life.

The Barrons would not have approved of my father's real self, so, loving my mother, he became somebody slightly different. Not quite a fraud, just a poorly sanitized forgery of who he'd been.

"And for what?" I said to my mother, listening to all this.

"For love," she answered. "For the sake of everybody's love."

My mother wasn't allowed to visit my father in the psychiatric wing, though she sat in the waiting-room lobby every day. She didn't mention Ben, who after all wasn't the cause of my father's problems, just a contributor. After two weeks, we decided it was time for me to go to Aunt Ida's on Sunday. Mom said she couldn't bear to yet. Whether she was exhausted or ashamed of her bad luck or had already somehow resolved to change her life, I don't know. But I was finally granted my job as ambassador, from the Savitz family to the Barrons.

I tried on a dozen outfits. Bright colors were too cheery; black was defeated. I didn't want to call attention to myself by breaking any of the Barron rules for clothing: no white, which was for nurses and brides, or jeans, which were for cowboys. I still had to please them. Finally I chose a blue skirt and blouse, and as I looked in the mirror I knew I didn't want to go to

Aunt Ida's, not ever again. But I had to. She would worry if I didn't.

The mood was a bit somber, though not enough for my taste. They were talking about a book they'd all read and eating an elaborate, dry-looking cake that Ida had made. They tried hard not to mention my parents.

About an hour into the afternoon, I couldn't take it anymore and announced that it was time for me to go home.

"Poor Sophie," Aunt Ida blurted.

I was clutching my purse. I nodded solemnly. "Poor us," I said. I meant it.

All the Aunts and Uncles joined in.

"Oh, Sophie," said Uncle Mose. "We're so worried for your mother."

"She's taking it very well," I said. "It's Dad I'm really worried about."

"Waiting for Frank to finally snap," Aunt Sadie said. "Hiding what she knew about him."

I put down my purse. I asked, "What did she know about him?"

The Aunts and Uncles looked at one another nervously. "Well, we all knew this would happen. I mean, with his history, it was bound to. You know," said Aunt Rose, "your father didn't ever finish his Ph.D."

"What?" I said.

"I know," said Aunt Sadie. "Terrible."

"No," I said. "I can't believe you're talking about him like this."

"How should we talk?" said Uncle Mose. His bright shirt, which once would have delighted me, just made me tired. "We're worried about our sister."

"What about your brother-in-law," I said.

"Him?" said Aunt Ida. She could not bear to use the word *brother-in-law,* and I realized: less than brother meant nothing, meant stranger. My father had just showed himself as what they'd known all along he was—not good enough for the Barrons, a nobody, a crazy.

"Now, your father is a wonderful man—" Aunt Ida began.

Uncle Mose snorted; Rose poked him.

"He's a *good* man," said Aunt Ida, and I could tell she thought good was better than wonderful. She picked up her plate, waiting for me to help her. But I couldn't.

"My father's suffering," I said.

"Yes, yes," said Aunt Ida. "But what kind of life will Esther have after all this? That's what eats me up. That's what I think about all the time."

"Jesus Christ, I can't believe you people," I said.

"Now, Sophie—"

"Sophie honey—"

"This is your fault," I said. "Can't you see that?"

There was a half-second pause. Aunt Ida bit her lip, wondering if this were so. Then Uncle Mose laughed, wisely. The Barron secret weapon. "Look, Ben was just doing your family a favor."

"A favor?" I echoed. "Losing our money?"

"He didn't know," said Aunt Rose.

"The deal was good, it just went bad," said Aunt Sadie.

"These things happen in real estate," said Uncle Mose. "Real estate is like that. Your father knew the risks."

"All for the best," said Aunt Ida, confident now. "Something was bound to happen sooner or later. All this—" She waved her hand, to indicate great nonsense; she was holding a piece of cake and some crumbs flew off. "Not good."

"What wasn't?" I asked.

"Your father," she said. "I mean, he was sooner or later going to fall apart. We saw; we knew. Your poor mother couldn't go on like that, worrying every day of her life about what would happen to her. Things might be bad now, but not as bad as they could be. I mean, how long could it have gone on?"

"Forever, if not for you," I told them. "And I wish to God it had gone on. That was my life that's been happening all these years."

My mother was in the kitchen when I got home, absentmindedly washing a dish, her back to me.

I said, "Aunt Ida says what's happened to Dad is all for the best. She says she knew it would happen." I took a deep breath. I shouldn't have said anything. I should have let the whole matter drop. "I hate those people."

One of her shoulders lifted, then the other one, slowly—not from dishwashing, but as if she were comparing the weights of two precious objects in her hands. I thought maybe she was just wondering how she'd gotten there, her hands wet, holding the plates that my father always took care of. Then the dish fell into the water with a plop, and she turned around.

She smiled. I was sure that, like any Barron, she would try to explain what had just happened and how it was unavoidable. Then she ran a wet hand through her hair.

What she said was, "Those *jerks*."

"Jerks?" I said, stunned.

"To treat you like that. No regard for you or your father and me. Jerks," she said again. Water dripped off her hands onto the floor.

And she made her feelings clear when Aunt Ida called that night. "I don't appreciate what you said to my daughter. Yes, you did say. You should have given some thought to us. No Ida, I am really mad. You stay out of my business."

You stay out of my business. How she got the nerve to say this to a Barron I still don't know. The claim that my mother's business did not belong to all of them, was not open to committee argument, meant only one thing to Aunt Ida: I do not love you anymore.

"She hung up on me," my mother said.

My mother, at age fifty, had taken her first step away from her family.

She sat down next to me on the sofa. "She's upset," she told me. "She was cooking soup, and she said I spoiled it."

"A tragedy," I said. "So she'll throw it out."

"So she'll throw it out," said my mother. "But. On the way to the sink, she slips. She spills the soup, gets covered in it. She breaks her leg."

"And the ambulance comes, and they see the soup," I said, "and they know they need to get her to the hospital, but what if the soup goes bad on the way?"

"It might kill her," said my mother. "They wrap her up in tin foil to keep her fresh."

"So they get in the ambulance, but on the way to the hospital, the drivers get distracted. Aunt Ida smells delicious."

"They just can't get chicken off their mind," my mother said.

"They stop at a roadhouse. Poor Ida is still in the back, but can you blame them? She smells like their mothers' kitchens."

"Nobody can blame them," I said.

"No," said my mother, and then, "Ida won't ever speak to me again, and over such a little thing."

I couldn't tell whether she was still playing the game or if this were a simple fact.

Aunt Ida and my mother had fallen down on the job. They forgot to dream of all the tragedies that now slipped, uncatalogued, into our lives.

My mother and I sat on the sofa picturing Ida in the ambulance, her slippery fragrant fingers smoothing her tin-foil stole. There she is, peering out at the stars through the little window in the back door, thinking about going into the restaurant to say something to the drivers, just a small, diplomatic reminder.

We loved her best then. We already missed her.

Three months later, still not speaking to my mother, Aunt Ida died of a heart attack.

"Broken heart," said Aunt Sadie, who called with the news. "Esther, you plain broke her heart."

How could this be so? Ida's heart had been broken so many times, she'd let it be broken. Uneaten ice cream, her daughter's smallest bad luck, a ruined dress, any tiny transgression. Surely all that heartache was good exercise, like push-ups; surely those little scars had made her heart tougher, used to abuse, maybe hungry for it. She could take grief. Hadn't she devoted her life to proving that?

Nevertheless, the Aunts and Uncles called my mother up to

announce this: they wouldn't be calling anymore. They'd had enough of her. They called one at a time, each trying to make it seem as though it had been his or her own idea.

"Foolishness," Mom said every time she hung up the phone. "I never heard of grown-ups acting this way."

My mother, the Barron, did not cry, was not sorry. Not sorry for what she had done. She didn't speak of her favorite sister's death, not for years, as if it were a final unforgivable snub.

My father came home, though he was never quite the same. He'd been given shock therapy at the hospital and developed an odd, intense look; he stared at people too directly. He lost his longing to invent things. His voice got soft, and people had to lean in to hear him. But he seemed to like that, a sudden tentative closeness.

And so my mother and father settled in to live the rest of their lives. Mom took on all the little jobs that Dad had taken care of before. I knew that in spite of everything, she still waited for the whole thing to blow over, for a single phone call.

When I was in high school, I had to write my obituary for journalism class; I remember it ended, "Miss Savitz is survived by her eight Aunts and Uncles." I was sure that they'd each stubbornly outlast the others, thereby outlasting me. I didn't know then that longevity was not a matter of pure will and logical argument. Ida was only first. Mose of a botched appendectomy; there goes Bram, of cancer. My mother, having cast off her Barron identity, is fine and lonely in the house with my father. She still tells stories of her childhood, full of the same nostalgia as always. When she talks about home, it's the house in Chicago she means, not where she is now, not my childhood home.

It's nowadays that I wish I'd inherited my father's longing for inventions, though I don't want to make lives longer or easier or speedier. There are inventions enough for that, and I'm not sure I approve of any of them. This is what I want:

There are these tourist traps—every state has one—Pilgrim Village or Wild West World or Alamo Days—where they re-create the past, and there are people in costumes and they pretend not to have ever heard of these times, our modern conveniences. I dream of doing that for Mom, of assembling Barron World, her childhood complete: look, there's the porch, and the horse that kicked Benny; there's the cranky piano player Sadie adored; there's Sadie, adoring him; and Bram, bookish, and Ida just getting over some tears, and your parents and the whole Barron set, unbroken, and you can just slip in, Mother, it will be like you never left.

THE GOINGS-ON OF THE WORLD

IN 1936 MY WIFE Rosie and I lived in a small town called Madrid, pronounced not like the town in Spain but with the accent on the first syllable, the vowel as flat and wide as the land around it—*Maaaa*drid. One morning in the last week of May I got up, got dressed, and killed my wife. I remember an argument the night before about oranges, and Rosie threatening to leave. I remember it was cold in that bed.

Afterward, on the front porch, I saw some pawprints in the lard that Rosie had set out for making soap. Raccoons. I couldn't recall which way town was. A few gray splinters dotted my hand, and my fingers didn't quite want to let go of the wooden handle. You know the ache of your arm when you put down something heavy, the ghost of weight still there? I feel that all the time, still.

The road I walked down, looking for somebody to catch me, smelled of chickens. I found my friend Nelson, a police officer. He took care of things. I pleaded guilty right away, and for that plea was sentenced to life instead of death, though believe me, those words aren't all that opposite. The past is like an old suit: you either put it on or get rid of it. Just looking doesn't tell you anything.

Now I live at Benson House, a halfway home run by the Cottage Grove Church. This is my second time out of prison. Reverend Massey, the minister in charge of Benson House, met me at Fort Madison and invited me, said I could stay forever if I wanted. So here I am, permanently halfway. He said I could earn my keep by washing dishes or cooking—now, how would I know how to cook? He's a nice young man with a beard, and the other men here—twelve of them—call him Dave. They call me Mr. Green, even Eddie, the cook, and we work in the kitchen together. Eddie came to Benson House four years ago as a guest, helped in the kitchen and got so good at it they offered him a permanent job. He's a skinny colored fellow who wears his hair in a number of braids, and when he takes me to the movies or out to the mall to walk around, we get looks. I'm in good shape for seventy-six, got my own teeth and my legs work, but next to Eddie I look frail. One time a guy with tattoos on his arm sidled up to us and asked if I was okay.

"Looks like a criminal type," the guy said, nodding at Eddie.

"Buddy," said Eddie. He took off his tweed cap and regarded the guy. "If you only knew."

Eddie takes care of me. He says, "Mr. Green, you need exercise," and we go for a walk. He sees a counselor twice a week and comes home with the leftovers. "You should keep a journal," he says. "You got a lot on your mind."

"Let it stay there," I tell him.

He shakes his head and the braids rattle. He says, "Not good."

The other fellows don't mention what I did, though they all know. I was in prison for so long that I got written up in the newspaper when I was released, both times. I'm a record holder. Most continuous years in prison in the state. Around here, in 1936, a life sentence meant just that—as long as you lived, no parole. But about 1984, the governor—who was four in 1936—got to thinking about me. He decided that I'd had enough of Fort Madison, or that Fort Madison had had enough of me, and commuted my sentence to ninety-nine years, which made me eligible for parole the next spring. The math of this eludes me, and I used to teach math. The reasoning went something like this: the laws had changed since 1936, and now fellows did what I did and worse, and got released sooner. I shouldn't, thought the governor, be a victim of my own bad timing.

Every night at Fort Madison, I dreamed up new ways to die. I slipped off the edge of a tall building or was torn into by an angry dog, or got shot in the woods by someone looking for food who bagged only skinny Joseph Green. One night I imagined undoing my body as if it were a machine, unscrewing first my feet, then calves, opening my torso like a cabinet and clattering around in there, untightening kidneys. Then, with an arm that in my dream still worked, I packed myself in a suitcase, veins and intestines coiled so that I would fit, muscles folded like bedclothes, lungs jigsawed together, and threw myself in the river.

My deaths took place outside the prison, every one. It was my way of keeping alive. I did not want to die there, forbade myself to even imagine it.

Because I was an educated man, Fort Madison gave me a job. As a watchman I earned three dollars a day, and saved it carefully—I didn't buy a TV when that was an option, read other people's old magazines. When I got out—seven thousand dollars rich—I had an idea I wanted to be an urbanite, so I climbed on a bus to Des Moines and found a room at a boardinghouse on the east side. There were a thousand things that I had not taken into account. I'm a well-read man—that's what the newspapers said at the time—and had kept up, I thought, with the goings-on of the world. The big things.

It was the small things that got me—the doors at the Hy-Vee that leapt away before I had a chance to push them, the way everything was packaged in gaudy, impossible-to-open containers. Almost all of the forty-nine years I had spent away were lost, great people obscure, ordinary people disappeared. I couldn't find shaving brushes or my favorite brands of candy; the light in stores was too bright by half; I ordered soup and a sandwich at a lunch counter and was asked to pay five dollars. The logic of things confounded me; I couldn't understand the simplest billboard. People's faces, close up, looked completely different, their skin a new texture, hair a new substance.

Women, especially, seemed weird, as if they were now manufactured differently. Let's be honest, it was a problem after those many years, all those bare legs and that long loose hair, unconcerned, looking fresh from bed. All of them out in the world: I stood on corners downtown and saw those girls flitting around, in groups together or with men. Salesgirls flirted with me, their fingers hit my palm when they handed me change. Sometimes they even winked. No one can tell me that's right.

I complained to my parole officer.

"You're like something H. G. Wells dreamed up," he said.

I disagreed; I didn't feel at all fictional. Just the opposite: I felt like the only real thing on earth, as if the new world was something I myself had inadvertently imagined, a detail a day for forty-nine years.

"People can tell about me," I told the parole officer. "They're frightened."

"*You're* frightened," he said. "Mr. Green, in this town what you did is just a drop in the bucket." As if I were flattering myself.

I wasn't ready for that life, thought maybe I never would be. I am not, believe me, a violent man by nature; my temper, when it kicks up, embarrasses me. I stole a box cutter from the grocery store, went to see my parole officer, that young man who, at the time, seemed to be the root of my problems. I went for his face, so that they'd see I was serious and dangerous—but I gave him time to put up his arms, and that's where I got him.

I was back at Fort Madison within a week, spent two more years there.

This time out, things are better. Plenty of good, if you know where to look—the headlights that flash into my window at night, all that perfume on people. I wake up at four-thirty, an hour before the other men, and get my own breakfast together. I've learned to boil eggs; yesterday, I looked down at one little egg in one little pan, the shell cracked, a bit of white in the water like the tail of a comet, and felt happy.

Sometimes I stroll down the street, with my head back to look at the sky, at night, early morning. I love to see the sun at the end of a day, resting its chin on the horizon, red and exhausted as a housewife. Last fall, when I was first out, I spent hours watching southbound birds move across cloudy skies that were solid and gray as cement. I supposed that on those overcast days the birds have to navigate by looking down instead of up, steering by streetlights instead of stars. I could almost see them hooking a wing, craning a neck: *Is that the river we passed last time, the highway, the filling station.*

And there's Eddie, and Dave Massey, and the people at the Cottage Grove Church, good people who sometimes even seek me out for conversation. I am taken care of, don't have to shop or go into restaurants or pay bills. I spend holidays at the church, eating meals in the function room downstairs with the other senior citizens who have nowhere else to go.

This is not to say that my life is without worry. For instance, three months ago, I went to the movies with Eddie. A red-haired actress played the girlfriend of the hero; she wasn't in much of the picture, but when she was, she reminded me of somebody. The recognition came in small stabs when she made one expression or another—I kept almost deciding who she was like, and finally, after an hour, I realized. It was Rosie. I had to leave the theater.

I sat on a bench in the lobby, shaking a little, furious but not knowing at who. I felt tricked.

Eddie came out.

"Mr. Green, you all right?"

The girl at the popcorn counter stared. I coughed and shook my head.

Eddie bought a fruit punch and a box of lemon drops. He sat down next to me.

"It's not a very good movie," he said. Then he took my hand and put a piece of candy in it. I ate fast, chewing down and letting the sugar get gummy in the cracks of my back teeth. Then I put out my hand for another. We sat there until the crowd came out of the theater, Eddie handing me lemon drops one at a time, me eating them as if they could dissolve the feeling of ash in my stomach. By the time we got to the car, I felt much better.

And most days I'm fine and can ignore the facts, tell my temper, Oh no you don't. I can take being a curiosity, like it even. Last fall, a television station decided that I was a Rip Van Winkle and sent a reporter over. She asked me slow, patient, rude questions. Did I do it? I said yes. Why? I didn't know. Did I believe in God? Sure, why not. Finally, she asked: of all the things I had seen so far on the outside—TV, computers, sex everywhere, the bomb—what amazed me most?

And I said: me.

At Fort Madison, I didn't think of my family; I didn't think of much. I concentrated on my watchman job, and on reading magazines, and on keeping clean, and on not dying. It was like I had killed everyone I ever met, like the people I once knew had simply disappeared, and I was not allowed to hear from them, or talk of them, or grieve for them.

Not hearing from my folks wasn't new: they'd cut off contact with me when I married Rosie. My family lived in Indianapolis; Madrid was Rosie's town.

My father was fond of saying, "Don't misunderstand me, but you're smarter than I am." He didn't mean it nicely. The last time he said it was at the dinner table the week I graduated from college.

"Educated man," he said, shaking his head.

He ran a furniture store and wanted me to take over, and none of my refusals, my petty transgressions, could dissuade him. I had tried politeness, rudeness, threats. At twenty-one, I burst into tears at breakfast; I crashed the family car; I was purposely careless with money. Nothing would change my father's mind.

My sister, Evelyn, was not expected to work in the store, since according to my father men didn't want to buy furnishings from girls. She had enrolled at Butler University the previous fall and had just started seeing the young man who would be her husband. Now she was giggly and harebrained all the time. I knew she would marry, that she would be allowed to belong to a different family, a different set of responsibilities. She sat at the dinner table and kicked the legs of my chair absentmindedly, her face already bright with that future. She would never have to work in that dusty store, full of people who wanted to quibble over prices, who searched for a scratch or a squeaky hinge, anything to pay a little less. Every thump of her foot reminded me.

"I can't work there," I told my father.

My father was examining his fork, trying to fix a bent tine. "Of course you can," he said. He looked at me and smiled.

"You don't care about family duty? Fine. This is a business transaction. You owe me. I'm collecting my debt."

The next week I drove to Madrid to visit a friend. Later, I learned that he wanted me to meet his sister, Irene, but I spent my time in the kitchen with Rosie Roach the hired girl. That's what the family called her always, the full name and the description, as if she were the heroine of a comic strip. She was Irish and freckled like the rice pudding she served, pale and cinnamoned. She got on well with my friend's family, and every time I snuck back to talk to her, she said, "Irene's looking for you," or, "She's a sweet girl, Irene," or "For God's sake . . ." But Irene was loud and gangly, with a nose shaped like the state of Nevada.

I wrote to Rosie after the visit and finally moved to Madrid to be with her, marry her. My father's letter said, "You have chosen this girl in order to disappoint us," and that might have been true. A family business, he called it that day at the dinner table, as if the store were a particular hair color or birthmark, or the shape of shoulders just like your father's, and denials could not shake it from you.

But marrying Rosie worked.

I'd been at Benson House for six months when Eddie called me to the phone.

"Western Union, Mr. Green," he said.

The Western Union lady's voice was all business as she said, "Dear Joseph. Will visit you August tenth at noon. Your sister, Evelyn. We'll send you a printed copy right away."

I waited a few seconds, not sure what part of the message was from Western Union and what from Evelyn. "They do it this way now, huh," I said.

"What?"

"By telephone. Takes the drama out somehow."

"We do it this way, sir," said the woman, and hung up.

I wondered whether Evelyn had telegrammed for the drama of it. I didn't know whether she was given to such stuff, though this wasn't the first I'd heard from her. In 1965, at Christmastime, I got a letter from her, my only sibling. It wasn't directly to me, actually—it was titled "Holiday Bulletin" and was addressed to "Dear Friends." It explained everything that had happened to Evelyn and her family in the past year, including this line: "Of course, most of you know that my father passed away this July. He was seventy-five." The letter had been duplicated on some kind of machine, and the blue words seemed projected onto the page, out of focus, not part of the paper itself.

The next Christmas I got another Holiday Bulletin, and the year after that a package besides, full of candied fruit and stale cookies, wrapped according to regulations (which meant she had called to find out). Evelyn kept up her side of the correspondence for the rest of my time at Fort Madison, never allowing me the luxury of a return address. The bulletins carried Indianapolis postmarks for the first few years and then started coming from Boynton Beach, Florida. I saved those letters and re-read them, soothed by the lists of relatives I had never known and never would, reports of weddings and births and the occasional death and never a mention of me.

When I got the Western Union call, Eddie stayed in the room and watched my face carefully. I never get phone calls, and he was worried. Eddie, like the other men here, is always a little scared, always thinks that someone is calling to say, We made a mistake. You have to come back now.

"My sister," I explained. "She's coming to visit me. Next week."

"You have a sister," he said.

"Younger," I told him. "I haven't actually spoken to her since 1935. Still haven't—that was a telegram."

"Well," said Eddie. He has family problems of his own, including a little boy who visits here now and then and never stops crying.

"It's good," I said finally. "I'm glad."

But the week was tense. Eddie lowered his voice in a superstitious way when he mentioned Evelyn.

"This lady, your sister," he said. "Don't let her upset you."

"Not me," I told him.

He was quiet a minute. "You don't talk about these things," he said. "Not healthy. You can't cure whatever's wrong by ignoring it."

"That's counselor crap," I told him. "Talk doesn't fix everything." I was mad at him, maybe the first time I ever was. But I was calm. "Eddie," I said. "Words are not it."

Whatever was wrong with me is still wrong with me. Whatever it is, it started that morning in 1936, when I woke up in our attic bedroom and the house was empty of its usual smells because Rosie Roach the hired girl had packed them all up with her clothing and the frying pans. She was sleeping downstairs, waiting for one of her boyfriends to come to the rescue. I told the judge I had nothing to say on the matter, and I still have nothing. I am not over it, I am not over it, I will never be over it.

Young people have a hard time believing that anything is permanent.

The morning Evelyn was set to come, I waited in my room. I didn't want to keep staring out the front window. Eddie poked his head in every now and then. He was sorry about our argument, and so was I, but too nervous to apologize. Because we worked for the house, we were the only ones home weekdays, with the other men at their jobs and Dave Massey at the church.

"Things okay, Mr. Green?"

I nodded.

"Going to be okay?"

"I expect so."

"I'll be around, you know, in case."

At two he knocked on my door frame.

"You have a visitor," he said formally.

My heart began to skitter in my chest like water on a hot grill. I was worried that it would evaporate completely.

I walked to the front sitting room, and there was Evelyn, an old woman already, old suddenly, and barnacled with rhinestones. They were everywhere: on her ears, on her fingers, on the odd plastic purse in her hand. They even clung, hard and gray, around the collar of her sweater. I felt a rush of pleasure in recognizing that she was dressed thirty years out of date: her old-fashionedness, and my recognition, were sweet, and my heart cooled a little.

"Well, Joseph," she said.

She stood up, shook my hand, and squeezed it. Then she looked uncomfortable for a moment.

"Have a seat," I said, pointing her to the dusty sofa that one of the church ladies, upon her death, had been kind enough to give us.

Evelyn looked at me, and I saw her readying for speech: the news of the past fifty years, the news of her life. I couldn't see anything of the Evelyn I had grown up with, a nervous but badly behaved girl who, unlike me, was not the hope of the family. This woman was calm and a little sloppy—her lipstick was put on bigger than her lips, and her hair was cut short and had no color to it. The face, which was sensible, did not match the fussy spangled sweater or the full flowered skirt that looked like they belonged to a much younger woman, and maybe they did—that is, to Evelyn thirty years before. What I saw was the Evelyn I got to know in the letters, a woman who, because she was in charge of the holiday correspondence, seemed to be in charge of the family and maybe the world. I felt like I was watching her on television. I was terrified of what she might say.

She said, "Do you remember the servants' stairs at the house at Williams Street?"

Williams Street was where our family lived. When we were small, Evelyn and I dragged wood crates to the top of the back stairs and used them as sleds; Evelyn's crate once bounced at the landing and she broke her collarbone.

"I still dream about thumping down those stairs," she said, "and when I wake up, I'm achy all over till I remember it was a dream."

Please consider these words: *do you remember*. They mean everything.

Do you remember is the game sweethearts and friends play,

and strangers from the same college who meet at the bus stop. Married people lead a life of it, I guess: *do you remember our meeting, our courting, our parting*. There is something so personal and lovely and casual in that line.

It was something that no one had said to me for fifty years.

"Those crates." I shook my head.

That afternoon, we remembered: the teacher at School #27 who had her nose broken by a boisterous boy; the children's room at the John Herron Art Institute; Portia Alberghetti, the Italian girl down the street who had webbed toes and showed them to anyone who'd ask; how we thought all Italians had webbed toes; Mae West; 5046L, which was our phone number; the revival that came to town one summer; being dragged by our father from the revival; "Brother, Can You Spare a Dime"; Aunt Fanny's pies, which tasted of metal; every knick-knack in our house and the stories that went with them. Such old, dear friends.

We remembered absolutely nothing that happened after 1935; nothing important at all. She worked my memory like it was a machine, saying *remember this,* and *this*.

Finally I said, "You're pretty brave, coming here to see me."

"You're telling me." She put a hand on her stomach. "I was so nervous I thought of slipping out the back way. I'm okay now," she added.

"So. How are you?"

"Well." She pursed her mouth. "My husband died."

When she said this, I recognized her for the first time. The little bit of the Evelyn I knew that was left showed itself, something fretful to her lips.

"When," I asked.

"Oh, about a month ago. He had a heart attack. So I put my home on the market and left Florida."

"Where do you live now?"

"I don't," she said. Her eyes were a little blurry, but the rest of her face was amused. "I'm on vacation. I'm driving places—every night, I send a postcard to my daughter that says, 'Here I am, don't worry, I'm safe.' " She looked up at me. "You're the only living relative who knows where I am."

All I could say was, "No kidding?"

Out of her strange bag she pulled a stack of postcards kept together with an elastic band.

"You know," she said suddenly, "you're still a very handsome man. I will note that on tonight's postcard."

"No kidding," I said again. "I always wondered if you ever mentioned me to your children."

"Yes." She laughed. "I'm sorry to say they're awfully embarrassed and refuse to tell the grandchildren."

This got my Irish up. So there I was, disappointing generations ahead of me. Still, I understood it a little.

Evelyn read aloud as she wrote on the postcard. " 'Dear Mandy. I am in the Midwest, visiting my brother, Joseph, who is a very distinguished man—' "

"I thought I was handsome."

" '—and is handsome besides. I am fine and will go on to Chicago tonight.' "

"Say that I say hello."

" 'Your Uncle Joseph sends his regards. Love, Mother.' "

It was the best letter I ever heard, not because of the handsome or distinguished, but because she awarded me "uncle."

I walked her to the car. From the back seat, which was filled with suitcases and laundry baskets and even an old ukelele, she pulled out two boxes and handed them to me.

The first was a big flat box with an unassembled fan, an orange price tag half scraped off in the corner.

"It seemed awfully hot," she said.

The second held a pair of old shoes.

"They were Dad's. He wanted you to have them, don't ask me why. They've been around awhile. Keep meaning to send them to you."

The shoes were oxblood oxfords, twisted very badly out of shape. My father had feet wide as an ax blade, and I suddenly remembered that his shoes were always too narrow; I saw him sitting in his chair after a long day at the store, rubbing his sore and mistreated toes.

"Oh, sweetie." Evelyn touched the corner of her own mouth, very tenderly. "All these years I thought of you as a ghost."

I pulled at my fingers. I smoothed my hair. I said, "But I'm not."

"No," she said, and I couldn't tell whether she was relieved or frightened. "You're not."

"Well," she said. "It's a long drive to Chicago." She stood on her toes like a girl, and kissed my cheek. "I'll send you a postcard."

"I'm not going anywhere," I told her.

"Used to think the same myself."

I opened the car door for her.

"Love you, Joe," she said.

I answered, "Me too."

She drove slowly down the street, her arm waving out the window till she turned the corner. I thought, There goes my sister.

I had the definite feeling I would never see her again. But it was fine.

The weather seemed strangely chilly for August, but then again I am not especially knowledgeable about weather, or seasons for that matter. I carried my boxes inside.

Eddie was standing in the front hall.

"You didn't introduce me," he said.

I shrugged.

"It's okay. How are you doing, Mr. Green."

"Well." My mouth felt full of mist. "Okay."

"Do anything for you?"

I looked at my boxes. "Yes. Could you ask somebody else to wash tonight? I think I'm going to turn in now."

He looked at his watch. "Four-thirty," he observed. "Sure you're okay?"

"Yes. Tired, that's all."

"Sure I'll ask. I know these visits. They can really drag you down. You sleep tight, Mr. Green."

"I will. See you in the morning."

"Count on it," he said.

In my room, I played all the old games. I reviewed our conversation, putting in what I wish I had said—a few morbid jokes, a few more truths. For instance, when she said at the car, I love you, now I answered with the actual words, and others besides: I miss you, dear, I wish I knew you.

The fan was a complicated affair—an oscillating pedestal fan, according to the box, three speeds. It was in a dozen pieces. I crept into the kitchen so Eddie wouldn't hear me and I got a knife.

As I worked on the fan, I thought of Evelyn running across the country, in hotel rooms with the ukelele, her own children a distant memory.

Eddie would disapprove. He says, "Don't run away from your troubles, because they'll sure as hell run faster." He says think about them, make decisions, and they'll go away.

In 1936, I was a handsome man, it's true.

In 1936, the judge squinted at a report and said, "I don't understand, was it an ax or a hammer?" and I answered, I was crying, "It was one or the other, sir, don't let's quibble," and a policeman laughed, then was embarrassed.

In 1936, a month before this, my father sent a letter that said, "You still have your whole life in front of you." That was true, too.

I still don't know what it was; the papers, when I got out, did not tell me.

These facts would not go away, not ever.

Finally, after an hour, I got the damn fan together. It was a gawky thing, but when I plugged it in, it worked. The sun hadn't set yet, but I turned down my quilt.

I placed the thing so that, in its oscillations, it would cool all of me: first toes, then up to my head, then back. I parked the shoes under my bed.

It got pretty cold during the night, and I woke up a few times shivering. Every time I did, I hunkered down under the covers, and watched the fan slowly turning its head like a long-extinct bird, patiently scanning the room, holding its judgment for morning.

Acknowledgments

My thanks to the James Michener and the Corpernicus Society, the Fine Arts Work Center in Provincetown, and the National Endowment for the Arts for their generous support. Thanks also to Karen Adelman, Karen Bender, Joshua Clover, Allan Gurganus, Bruce Holbert, Sue Miller, Rob Phelps, Max Phillips, Pike Porter, Henry Dunow, Susan Kamil, Karen Rinaldi, Jason Kaufman, Deb West, and especially Ann Patchett. And, of course, thanks to my family.